T0000146

IN MOONLAND

Miles Allinson is a writer and an artist, and the author
of the multi-award-winning novel *Fever of Animals*
(Scribe, 2015). He lives in Melbourne.

IN MOONLAND

MILES ALLINSON

SCRIBE

Melbourne | London

Scribe Publications
18–20 Edward St, Brunswick, Victoria 3056, Australia
2 John St, Clerkenwell, London, WC1N 2ES, United Kingdom
3754 Pleasant Ave, Suite 100, Minneapolis, Minnesota 55409, USA

Published by Scribe in Australia and New Zealand 2021
This edition published in North America 2023

Copyright © Miles Allinson 2021

All rights reserved. Without limiting the rights under copyright reserved above, no part
of this publication may be reproduced, stored in or introduced into a retrieval system, or
transmitted, in any form or by any means (electronic, mechanical, photocopying, recording
or otherwise) without the prior written permission of the publishers of this book.

The moral rights of the author have been asserted.

Lyrics on p. 7 from 'Brothers in Arms' used with the kind permission of Mark Knopfler.

Printed and bound in the UK by CPI Group (UK) Ltd, Croydon CR0 4YY

Scribe is committed to the sustainable use of natural resources and the use of paper products
made responsibly from those resources.

978 1 957363 71 4 (US edition)
978 1 925322 92 7 (Australian edition)
978 1 922586 03 2 (ebook)

Catalogue records for this book are available from the National Library of Australia.

This project is supported by the Victorian Government through Creative Victoria.

This project is the outcome of a State Library Victoria Fellowship.

scribepublications.com.au
scribepublications.co.uk
scribepublications.com

For my mum, Margaret Halliday
And for Pardeshi and Rick

I knew nothing, and I persisted in the faith that the time of cruel miracles was not past.

STANISLAW LEM — *Solaris*

PART ONE

1.

In March 1996, a few months before he drove into a tram stop, my father bought an old Ford Torino with the money he'd won on a horse called Holy Moly. He was a fast, erratic driver, and it made him happy for a while, that car — the roar of it, the faded yellow phoenix on the black bonnet, the way the road seemed to open up for him. He hated traffic, but when all the lights are green, you can slide through the universe like a spirit without a body. Then things started to go wrong, and he had to spend a lot of money trying to fix them.

I was seventeen years old when it happened. My sister, Tara, was a year younger. Our mother was away at a yoga retreat. At the time, I don't think any of us really believed he was trying to kill himself. What he was trying to do, we assumed, was crash and claim the insurance. That was the sort of thing he would have done, and in fact, I half recalled him saying something to that effect once. Even now, so many years later, I still sometimes believe this to be the truth.

In any case, my father died before we could ask him what he'd been thinking. But I also know that it's possible to think or feel a number of contradictory things at the same time and to act decisively anyway. Maybe he didn't know which of the possible outcomes he preferred, death or insurance, maybe they were both okay in that moment, and what he really wanted was the thrill of sudden fate bearing down on him again. He was forty-three years old. I think he had been unhappy for most of my life.

About twenty years after he died, I became a father myself. It was a pretty tough labour — though I didn't do most of it, obviously — and I must have fallen asleep for a few seconds soon after my daughter's birth, because I can remember waking in fear at the edge of the hospital bed, confused, as if I had been lying on the floor of the ocean for decades and was only now being dragged back into the air.

I was in shock, and I think I remained in shock for a long time while I came slowly to understand just how definitively sundered I was from my former life. How lost, now, all those days and years were that preceded Sylvie's arrival. That period of my life was gradually becoming mythological. Or at least, it might seem like that to her, I thought, when she's old enough to imagine it.

Parents are only there to be memories for their children, Matthew McConaughey says at the beginning of *Interstellar*, a very frustrating film that's more or less forgotten now, and which I liked a lot for about an hour and a half when I saw it with Sylvie's mother, Sarah, a few days before Sylvie was born. In one scene, McConaughey leads his team of astronauts to an unknown water-covered planet, where they are hoping to find news of an earlier, doomed mission. And indeed, not far from where they land, the crashed remains of that first spaceship are soon found bobbing in the ocean, still surprisingly intact despite the many years that separate the two expeditions. Due to some sort of trick involving complicated physics and wormholes, a few simple moments on this watery planet are equivalent to a whole year on earth. Though it's taken them years to reach him, the first astronaut would have landed and died only hours earlier. Disaster quickly ensues. The mountains, which can be seen on the horizon, suddenly begin to approach. But they are not mountains. It's a giant wave that's been building for miles and which nearly kills them all, thrashing the spaceship and flooding its engine. Delayed in his return to the mothership, which is parked in space somewhere on the other side of the wormhole, McConaughey arrives back to find that years have passed. On earth, his children have grown up. In little more than an hour, he has become, for them, just a distant memory.

My own daughter will remember certain things about me, I thought as we left the cinema that night. *She will remember things that haven't even happened yet, but what will my previous life mean to her? All those moments up until now? And what about my own father's life before I was born? Where did that all go?* How little remained of that, besides a few unreliable anecdotes and a box of discoloured photographs with their vague aura of recklessness. So little, and less with each day.

A lot happened over the next year or so. Sylvie became — quite slowly at first — a delightful person, although Sarah and I eventually agreed to separate. We agreed, and then we agreed not to, and then we disagreed completely, although neither of us knew what to do about it, and we continued living together because the alternative seemed too horrible and too complicated. They say babies sense everything, that they are basically psychic, and maybe that's true, because even at the age of two, Sylvie was still waking five, six, seven times a night. We had tried to move her into her own room, and then we relented and let her come back into ours, so that during those periods when Sarah and I actually slept in the same bed, Sylvie slept between us, like a sacred rock that we worshipped and despised. Some nights, especially during that first year, she wouldn't sleep at all — none of us would sleep — and we would put her in the car and drive through the empty suburbs, past the same blazing 7-Elevens, the same ugly new apartment blocks.

I didn't think a lot about my own father during this period. I noticed him at the periphery of my thoughts, like you sometimes notice buskers on the street, and maybe I even threw him a coin every now and then — whatever that means — though I rarely stopped to listen. Then one day I went to the funeral of an old school-friend who had died suddenly, and who happened to share my father's name: Vincent. It was weird to hear his name spoken again, in such a context. It was also a terrible funeral. Nothing that was said even *approached* the mystery of the human life we were attempting to celebrate. People say 'celebrate', but they don't really mean it. Or they don't know what they mean. The priest went cheerfully through the motions, the same tired clichés no one believed anymore rolling off his tongue in a tone of heartbreaking complacency. Religion denies the weight of life, I once heard someone say. If it had been my child's body in that casket, I would have stormed the altar; I would have torn the hair from the priest's head. As it was, it was only my old school-friend's body. The ghost of my father's ghost. People filed up obediently for communion, while two screens hanging on either side of the altar displayed images from my friend's life. I saw him standing beside some sort of temple that had been carved into the side of a mountain. He was older than I remembered him to be. Of course. He was nearly forty. He was my age. Someone had pressed play on a Dire Straits song. *Through these fields of destruction*, Mark Knopfler muttered. My old friend was in a jungle in Cambodia. He was at Machu Picchu. He was in Brazil. He stood amid some tiered green hills in a place that might have been Vietnam. Then my old friend was standing in front of that stone doorway again, in India, I guessed. He was looking into the distance beyond the frame, not unaware of the camera, but seemingly unconcerned by it, absorbed instead, perhaps, by the magnificence of the place in which he had found himself. But I had seen that stone temple in another photo, I realised. It must have been a famous tourist attraction, because my father had stood there once himself, many years earlier, in a dirty orange robe.

That old photo of my father had disturbed me, when I found it among his boxes after he died. It had been taken the year before my parents met, apparently, in 1976, when my father's hair was thick and dark, and he had a big Frank Zappa moustache. My father had stayed for a couple of months in an ashram somewhere in India, according to my mother, although that was before her time, she told me. She didn't know much about it.

That story had taken me by surprise when I first heard it. My father was not a religious person. I had never known him to set foot in a church, let alone in an ashram. He'd hated his own father, who'd been a Methodist minister, and it was impossible to imagine my father praying to anyone. He was not a joiner or a meditator or someone you could imagine chanting or swaying or doing whatever they did in an ashram in India. He was a man of the physical world. As long as I could remember, he had worked for himself as a carpenter and as a builder, and, more generally, as a handyman, though no one taught him how to do any of it. He had taught himself, and he was good at it. He built things to last. If anything, he over-engineered them, as if he was afraid they would fall apart as soon as he turned his back. He did not trust that things would stay together. He did not trust authority, either. He hated authority. He swore at the television every time a politician opened their mouth to speak. He had strong hands, and tattoos of skulls on his arms. He liked to gamble and to drink and to win against the odds, even if it meant cheating, and, on more than one occasion, I'd seen him threaten to smash someone's face in with a hammer. And if you were to ask me what sort of father he had been, I would say that he was a good one, that he'd loved us, though I also know that I was terrified of him, that he had a rage we all feared, and that he was a troubled person, with a loneliness that could not be cured.

Above all, my father had seemed extraordinarily happy in that photo, and this, too, did not fit any idea I had of him. He was smiling in a way that I'd never seen him smile in real life. I'd never seen *anyone* smile like that. Much more than the robes or the hair, it was that smile that made the image strange: my father's extraordinary happiness.

But what had happened to that photo? We'd lost track of it in the weeks after he died, amid the numb chaos of funeral arrangements and police interviews. It had been too strange to even contemplate. I pushed it away and forgot about it. Suddenly, more than twenty years later, it had returned.

It took me a second to realise that I was the one who was whispering out loud. The images beside the altar changed again. My old friend was standing somewhere else now. The slideshow repeated itself. *What are these moments?* I kept thinking to myself. The priest was still speaking, but people were turning to look at me. *What are these images? Can religion ever approach them?*

Driving home that day, I nearly ran into the back of a RAV4. And that's when I had the idea to visit my father's old friends, the ones who were still alive. Banked in traffic, in grey light, on Punt Road yet again, I thought about those names from my childhood, my father's supposed friends: Abbie, Charlie, Denis. Names tethered to flashes of memory, to photos, rooms, gestures, admonishments, strange excursions in cars to who knows where. Names that flared up every now and then. Who were these people, and what did they know about my father that I didn't know? Maybe I could ask them what sort of person he had been. Who was he? What were the moments that survived? Out of fear, my father had remained a mystery to me. I was afraid to unwrap the forgetfulness that held him where he was: vague, embalmed, harmless. That's how it all started. I didn't expect things to turn out the way they did.

2.

Our mother's name was Catherine Kelly, and she made a point of remembering almost nothing from our childhood, or of remembering only in quick clichés that couldn't possibly be true. She was in a fog for most of it, she once told me, and there are days I still half-wonder whether we even had a childhood at all, Tara and me, or whether that old beige leather folder of family photographs wasn't actually fabricated, like those photos in *Blade Runner*, which were handed out to Replicants to augment their artificial memories. Staged holidays. Photoshopped birthdays. Who were those naked children and those animals they seemed to love so much, those rabbits, that endless supply of cats and birds? Nor did our mother remember much from her own childhood, it seemed. She rarely spoke about her own family unless we pushed her.

Between us, over the years, Tara and I had assembled some rudimentary family knowledge. Our mother grew up poor in rural Victoria, the youngest of three sisters, hoping for many years that she would be a saint like Joan of Arc. Once, when she was nine, an angel came and stood in her bedroom, huge and androgynous. Her parents were bitter, obedient Catholics. Her father worked in the canning factory, though he dreamt of being a farmer one day, living on a Catholic commune somewhere even bleaker than where they already lived. But her mother didn't want to do that, understandably, and it never happened. My mother survived, is what she felt, I think. She got away. She went to university, and lived in a series of big communal houses, and met people who were interested in politics and music. She became a mystery to her parents, it seemed, an aberration. And then they died, in quick succession, before she had even finished her undergraduate degree. She was not close with her sisters — politically they had nothing in common — and apart from a few dismal Christmases together as small children — long, strange, sun-blasted days in rural Victoria — Tara and I hardly ever saw our cousins. I don't know how other people feel about their own family history, but it always felt to us, I think, as if something was missing.

Our mother wanted to be a singer like Joni Mitchell, who she faintly resembled, when she met our father at a full-moon party in 1978, at his house, in Byron Street, in Elwood. That's how the story goes. A full moon in Taurus. The house belonged to our father then. Soon it would belong to our mother too, and then to me and Tara, in that order. Now it's simply a façade that belongs to someone else. The rest is gone. The rest is just jutting glass and concrete. I cannot stand the music of Joni Mitchell. She annoys the shit out of me.

It's that house that convinces me we did, in fact, have a childhood, and in dreams I'm often still there. Or I can close my eyes and run my hand along the long hallway walls. I know the cracks off by heart, the bits of thick paint, the gouges in the plaster where something or other happened. I don't remember what happened, but I remember where. Or sometimes I do remember what happened, and then I'd rather not. This is where my father threw a plate, a glass, a whatever. This is where he smashed that thing I loved. This is where he kicked the door off my bedroom, or threw the television against the bookcase.

He liked throwing things.

Tara fought him. She was stronger than me, in that sense. She stood her ground and growled back at him. Or screamed. She slammed more doors than me. He never hit her. He never hit any of us, not really, though I think he came very close many times. Like the day he ripped out the rangehood from above the stove with his bare hands while my mother was cooking. Like the day he put an axe through the fridge. 'You got shit for brains?' he would say, smashing something against something else. 'Don't you understand anything?' But he was right. We didn't understand. Afterwards, he would pretend that nothing had happened. He would become cheerful, patient, kind. A loving father. He would put things back together again, which was a bit annoying for him, of course. Our silence seemed to mystify him. In the case of the fridge, for instance, or the television, he went out and bought another one.

My mother wanted to be a singer, but instead she became an Arts student, and then a nurse, and then, after my father died, a property manager. But in the very early seventies, she was a backing singer, briefly, for a band called The Acapulco Astronauts. They released one record, *Sounds from Beyond and Beyond the Beyond*, which I can remember listening to as a child, sitting in afternoon light on the green carpet in our back room. It was hard to know which voice was my mother's, and I didn't like the music much — its faux sentimentality confused me — but I liked the album cover, or, at least, I often used to stare at it, wanting to like it, because my mother was on it and she looked beautiful to me and disturbing. She was dressed in red, and she was gripping a cigar in her teeth and leaning on a Tommy gun, as if it were an umbrella. In the days of the Astronauts, as she occasionally referred to them — the pre-me days, in other words — my father seemed to know people: musicians, artists, filmmakers, record producers, none of them very good, it turned out, or very influential, but maybe these connections were part of his appeal. Maybe our mother thought he could help her career. In any case, he didn't, and nothing came of any of it, I suppose. Our mother let it go in the end, that dream she had of stardom. That world disappeared into another, into the world of the family, though sometimes, when she had been drinking, she would sing in a high, clear, sad voice that I loved and was also ashamed of. It sounded to me as if she were trying too hard. There was something desperate about it. But then she began to go deaf and stopped singing altogether.

Our parents were married against their own parents' better judgement. Our father's father was a Methodist minister, as I've mentioned. Tara and I only met him a handful of times. He was a large, funny, cruel man who spent the last years of his life alone and drunk in a caravan on the edge of a town called Katamatite, a couple of hours' drive from Melbourne. The local football team had gained some notoriety many years earlier, when they defeated the neighbouring town of Wattville 78.19 (487) to 1.3 (9), but this seemed to be the place's single defining feature. Our grandfather had disliked my mother for her Catholicism, and didn't come to the wedding, a simple, irreverent ceremony in the backyard in Byron Street — there were photos — without shoes and with a lot of marijuana (you could see the giant crops in the background). They were a sweet-looking, nervous couple. Almost happy, it seemed. They had not known each other long, and they appeared to be waiting for the significance of the moment to dawn on them. My father in brown flares and a yellow shirt. My mother pregnant with me. They held hands as they cut the small cake. Our father's mother was an art teacher and a painter, a distant sort of woman, who liked to believe she was descended from Spanish aristocracy. She was at the wedding, too, looking frail and dainty and uncomfortable on the low bamboo couch, but she died soon afterwards, before I was born.

Tara and I were both born before our parents realised how little they had in common, I think. Or how fundamentally their misconceptions had been betrayed. Or perhaps we helped reveal these misconceptions; perhaps we triggered some bomb that had been lying in wait, and which caused them each to change and move away from each other, to retreat into their own bitterness. They fought, but not often or outrageously. Our mother tended to withdraw, to wait out the storm. Sometimes I would find her sitting in the huge yellow Kingswood that was our car then, reading or crying. She kept a book called *Lives of the Saints* in the car for such occasions, which she also read at the traffic lights, sometimes, while she was driving. And yet our parents stayed together. They even loved each other. They stayed together, and they kept renovating the house, as if that might fix other things.

Our father built a lot of that house himself — the illegal extensions, at least — and he still occupies it in my dreams. An old, semi-detached brick Victorian house. When my mother finally sold it, she did so because she felt it was my father's body she was living in, or a tomb for his body, or a tomb she had been left to carry around on her back, like some sort of creature that clings to your head and blinds you — a monstrous pangolin, for instance, or some sort of chimera. So she sold it, and she washed her hands of it, and we moved into an apartment for a little while, just the three of us — a period of derangement and freedom — in another suburb on the other side of the city. Our mother practised self-hypnosis and took up smoking again, and we each drank ourselves into other worlds. Finally, Tara and I moved out into our own lives, and our mother quit smoking for a second or third or fourth time, met a man called Bill Ventura, married him, and moved to the Gold Coast, where the blinding glare of the sun erased almost everything. That's where they lived for a long time, on the seventeenth floor of a monstrous white apartment complex. I say this without snobbery. With only a trace of snobbery. I watched a storm from the large windows of that apartment one Christmas, a tremendous black mist crossing the ocean towards us. I understood the appeal of those windows.

After Sylvie was born, I used to talk to my mother on the laptop every Wednesday and Sunday, so that she could read a story to Sylvie and stay known to her. She was not what you would have called a hands-on grandmother. She was what you might have called a hands-free one. She was afraid of flying, she said, because it takes at least a day for the soul to catch up with the body. She sent Sylvie crystals in the mail, and worry dolls, which were choking hazards, and books about frightened unicorns who find their voices.

'What was Dad like when you met him?' I would sometimes ask, and she would say something vague. 'Oh, you know, he had something about him,' and then she would fiddle with her hearing aid as if I were cutting out. Invariably, I would remember then the afternoon, as a child, when I saw her walking past the schoolyard where I was playing. What was she doing there? And why didn't she come over and say hello? I remember clinging to the wire fence and calling out, and how she did not turn around. But she must have heard me. She was carrying a colourful shopping bag. She kept walking. She crossed the road carelessly. I remember the back of her head that was suddenly unknown to me, her pale hair bright in the sun, and then she disappeared around a corner, and a teacher, who I did not like, carried me away.

3.

Sylvie turned one. Then she was one and a half, and I still hadn't spoken to any of my father's old friends. I had other things on my mind, although, it's true, I did sometimes go out of my way to drive past the old house in Byron Street, renovated beyond recognition, but still there, more or less. The big gumtree, gone. The fence with my name scrawled across it a thousand times, gone. The garden gone. The little glinting view through the front window into my parent's bedroom still, technically, there. A few times I sat in the car out the front with the engine running until someone came out of the house, and then I'd drive off like a criminal. An amateur criminal. Speaking of amateur criminals, I would think, who *was* my father, the man who had stolen the materials to build so much of that house, and then built it? That dodgy gambler. That bastard. He had been dead twenty years, and I still had the sudden urge to get away from him.

But he was also perfect. A lovely giant. So kind and funny. So good with children, so generous. And such a good storyteller.

Other times he would be something else again, something far too close to be seen clearly. In which case he was not Vincent, not my father or my Dad, not even mine. He was me, somehow, or I was him. *His body in my body*, I would think, amazed, repulsed.

But what does it mean to live for a while and then kill yourself one Friday just because you feel like it? Or because you have gambling debts? Or because you're depressed? Or because you want the insurance? Or maybe because you just like driving really fast? He drove up one of those yellow dividers that used to separate the tram-stops from the road, and flipped.

He didn't leave a letter, that's the thing. Nothing, not even a note on the pad next to the phone: *I just like driving really fast. Sorry. Back soon, unless I'm not. In which case, I love you all.*

Which he did, for the record. He loved us all. Though love is terrible, as everybody knows.

I was talking to my mother over the computer one Sunday, with Sylvie on my lap. That night she read a story about three little owls whose mother disappears. *She'll be back soon*, the little owls keep telling each other. *Very soon*, they say. And then, because I asked, my mother told me again how she and my father had met through a mutual friend, at a full-moon party one night in 1977. My father had just got back from Asia, 'very dashing and tanned', and he still had an aura about him, my mother said — 'a terrific kind of radiation' — that drew her to him. 'He was a beautiful man,' she said, and for a little while it felt like they could do just about anything in the world together.

Terrific radiation? Was she drunk? My mother hardly ever spoke about my father, even when prompted, and certainly not to tell me how terrific his radiation was. *Terrific* was a Bill word. I didn't know where *radiation* came from.

'What?' I said. 'Terrific *what?*'

'Sure,' she shrugged, 'why not? They were both terrific, him and Abbie.'

'Abbie?' I was confused. I hadn't heard about Abbie in twenty years. 'Did Abbie set you guys up or something?'

'No,' my mother said. 'I met them both at the same time. They were like a team, the two of them. They came back together.' She fiddled with her hearing aid. 'I'm not sure where they met,' she said vaguely. 'But look, Joe, what's your heating situation down there? Because it looks awful, and those blow heaters are incredibly expensive to run.' Now she had that look in her eyes that I recognised. She was disappearing again.

I could hear Bill Ventura clanking around somewhere off-screen. Terrific old Bill. He managed a car-hire company and took photos of sunsets on the weekend with a telescopic lens.

'Do you have Abbie's phone number?' I asked.

'Gosh, I don't think so,' my mother said, finishing her white wine in a way that signalled the end of the conversation. 'I don't know where that would be.'

Sylvie was clutching at the screen.

'Goodnight, little owl,' my mother said to her, squeezing up her face.

—

But my mother *did* have Abbie's number, it turned out. She texted it to me the following night, without comment, and two days later I sent him a text of my own.

I waited, but I got nothing in return. And so, a week after that, I called. I didn't expect him to answer. I thought he was probably dead.

4.

'G'day Abbie, it's Joe, how's it going?'

A pause.

'Ahh, Brat.'

Brat was the name he'd called me as a teenager. Never Joe.

'I was just ringing because. Did you get my message? I was wondering if you felt like having a chat about Dad sometime.'

'Yeah, right,' he said.

It was a voice I knew so well. I thought of the night he'd come back to Melbourne, prodigal somehow, dragging behind him that hint of scandal. That would have been 1993, a good year as far as I was concerned. The year *Jurassic Park* was released. The year Essendon won the Premiership, from nowhere. I was fifteen years old. We were eating dinner. Without knocking, Abbie simply strolled into the house, sat down at the table, and began helping himself. My mother burst into tears. 'You shit,' she said, getting up to hug him. My father laughed nervously, but soon enough he was leaning back in his chair, telling jokes, as if something in him had been released.

Abbie was an unhurried, handsome American, with greying blonde hair and eyes like bright water. That's how I remembered him. An exceptionally handsome man, actually, despite the nose that had been bashed in years ago. In America he'd been in movies, though none of them very good, apparently, and it was impossible to find them in the video store. According to Dad, he was friendly with the actor Terence Stamp, who played an evil alien in an old Superman movie. Tara, I think, fell in love straight away. Or at any rate, she quickly switched her allegiance from whoever she was obsessed with at the time, to him. What he had been doing up north was never clear. And what did that even mean, *up north*? Abbie chuckled when I asked. I guess I liked him, too, if for no other reason than because we were allowed to watch *The Simpsons* when he was around. He loved *The Simpsons*. During the next two years, until my father died, Abbie was always at our place. He spent Christmases and birthdays with us, and occasionally I would come home to find him reading my Phantom comics, lying on my bed with his dirty feet. *Don't mind me*, he'd say, but he wouldn't get up. Maybe he flirted with my mother. Maybe there was something conspiratorial about his friendship with my father. I imagine them plotting something mildly illegal. In any event, Abbie's presence brought a holiday atmosphere to those last years, just as the beginning of summer charges the air with expectation. One day he arrived on a motorbike, which I never saw again. The rest of the time he drove a golden BMW with a cracked windscreen. Unlike my father, though, he was never in a hurry. Behind the wheel he was somehow disinterested, as if he had more important things on his mind than the road itself. Unlike my father, he never yelled at the other drivers, or veered violently from lane to lane, or picked fights in my company.

He never leapt from the car with the steering-lock in his hand. And yet Abbie had been wronged somehow — this I gathered gradually — and he held grudges against a long list of people I'd never heard of.

Also, it was Abbie who came to tell me what had happened to my father. That he'd rolled his car up a tram stop. That he was in hospital. That he was dead. I was in my final year at high school. My name was called over the loudspeaker. I came out of the classroom, and saw Abbie standing in the middle of the hallway, near the office. A crowd of students was trying to get past him. He didn't move. I couldn't figure out why he looked so weird. He tried to smile, but there was something wrong with him.

We went and picked up Tara from her school. Then he drove us both to the hospital. We did not speak; or maybe we did, but I have no memory of what we might have said, none, just a sense of Abbie's solidarity beside me, and of the buildings we passed: the oblivious glass shopfronts, a bakery, a milk bar, a bottle shop, none of which exist anymore. Abbie didn't speak at the funeral either; he wasn't asked, I suppose, though I don't know why he wouldn't have been, or he declined, and after the funeral, he moved back north without saying goodbye. The last time I had seen him was the day after the funeral. He was cleaning up, collecting beer bottles and cigarette butts. So, it was weird to hear his voice again now, and I found myself adopting the tone I remembered my father having used — wry and playful, comically masculine. The flicker of a smile in it. I hadn't thought of that tone for a very long time, because he only ever used it with Abbie. In fact, I had the disconcerting feeling that my father was using me to speak again, as if he had sensed his chance, somehow, and was rushing through my body to seize it.

But then this feeling was shot down.

I realised, too slowly, that Abbie was saying no. He didn't want to try and remember the seventies. He didn't want to talk about my dad. He didn't really want to speak to me, either.

'I don't think I'd be very enthusiastic about doing that,' he said. 'Nah.'

The silence buzzed.

'Can I ask why?' I heard myself say, in my own diminished voice again.

'Well,' Abbie said, drawing out the word good-naturedly. 'All that stuff's finished now, isn't it? None of it matters anymore.'

'None of it matters?' I said. 'To who? To you or to Dad?'

It was a nonsensical question. I sounded vaguely hysterical.

'Well, certainly to him, that's for sure,' Abbie said, more kindly than he might have. 'And for me. I mean all that stuff's been a bit mythologised, I reckon.'

I had no idea what he was talking about. But isn't that the purpose of friendship — not only to mythologise, but also to understand the truth of the myth?

Abbie suggested I speak to Denis, and to Charlie if he was still around.

I told him to call me if he changed his mind. But he didn't call, and in fact, soon after this conversation, he left Australia for good. He moved to India and never came back.

5.

Discouraged, it took me a while to get back to it, after Abbie. Winter came. At home, the heaters hummed all day, and the warm air was met perfectly by the freezing air that came through the cracks in the floorboards, and nothing was changed. The rooms remained bearably, expensively cold.

For the first two years of Sylvie's life, we lived in that crappy house, with its big empty lawn and some lovely old Greek neighbours who were always passing something over the fence to us, plates of miscellaneous meat, mostly. They could not believe that Sarah was a vegetarian. There was no such thing, as far as they were concerned. I ate it all for a while, Sarah's share and mine, until I started dreaming of meat, of abattoirs, of thick stews of feet and gizzards, and then I couldn't do it anymore. I felt nauseated just looking at it. I tipped it all straight into the bin. *Delicious*, I would say. *Amazing. Thank you!* Sometimes the little old husband would come through the rain to knock on the door and wake the baby with another plate of dead bodies. *Thank you, thank you. But please, my god, if you ever wake the baby again I will fucking murder you.*

Of course they didn't know what was going on, that Sylvie would startle at the slightest noise, that it took hours to get her back to sleep, that she would cry and cry and cry, that we were mad. 'Bring the baby,' they would complain. 'Why you no bring the baby?' *Of course. Of course*, we would say. But the baby reeled away from them in horror, and we would snatch her back, and make some excuse, and retreat behind our fence again.

Walking the pram in the freezing dark very early one day, the thought hit me — a procession of thoughts really, though they felt at the time like a single, united blow, like someone slugging me from behind — *what am I doing on this corner at the end of the world? Who am I? Who are* you, *for that matter, baby? And why do I live in this awful suburb?*

Is this how my own father felt when I was born? I wondered. As lost as this? Like his future had been erased? Like his life had shrunk to the size of a blackened pea? I walked home and stood in the backyard and did not know what to do. Everything seemed alien, meaningless. The low sky. The backyard with its frosted lawn and plastic garden furniture. The garage stuffed to the ceiling with more plastic garden furniture and boxes of things I had forgotten about but couldn't throw away, with tools that had belonged to my father, and which I did not know how to use.

It was six-thirty in the morning. I crept in quietly through the back door so as not to wake Sarah. I put Sylvie in her highchair and gave her something to eat. I knelt under her chair, picking up tiny, disgusting pieces of food from the floor. She reached out and took a handful of my hair in her grimy fingers, laughing delightedly. I cleaned her, I changed her nappy, and then I walked down the hallway and placed her on the bed in the darkness beside Sarah. I opened the blackout blinds. There was a steel grille over the window that made the room even gloomier, and which I'd vowed to remove, though I knew in that moment that I'd never get round to it. Sarah was not asleep after all. She'd been lying awake since two in the morning, she told me. Her eyes were red; her face was streaked with tears. She said something that I can't remember, although somehow everything seemed to be my fault. I had failed in some way that wasn't clear to me. I didn't say anything. I kept very still and tried to understand what I was feeling. But I didn't understand it. Life is mysterious. Hatred is mysterious. Then I caught the train to work. Out the window, in the winter sun, the bare stretches of highway seemed to me as lovely as water.

That morning, I sat at my desk and finished a couple of press releases I'd been too tired to finish the day before. Then I interviewed a professor about his research in drone technology. The university had begun offering drone-pilot training as part of a degree, making 'unmanned aviation' available to the service industry. *The future is coming*, I wrote. In fact, the future was already here. It was being secretly funded by corporate weapons manufacturers. It was called Surveillance Capitalism. I didn't write that. I fiddled with the website. I tweeted and retweeted, although since I'd been promoted — from Communications Advisor to *Senior* Communications Advisor — I'd handed over most of the social media to Bec.

It was a good job most of the time, I should say that. It was fine. I liked the team, the research was interesting, and it was certainly more satisfying than the supermarket where I'd previously worked, managing internal comms, and where *prices were always down down*

down! And yet, exhausted as I was, it was sometimes hard to know if anything I was doing was real. I was itchy with fatigue, and often fell asleep at my desk and dreamt tiny, alarming dreams. That afternoon, I dreamt of a house surrounded by a black forest. I dreamt I found my guard dog mauled almost to death by wolves. Her guts had spilt out onto the wet grass. I was forced to slit her throat with a razor blade. When I woke up, I was still holding my coffee above the keyboard. Bec was staring at me with that look of hers: pity mingled with fear. I smiled at her and decided to call Abbie again. Then, remembering his advice, I decided not to. Speak to Denis, he'd told me. So I did. I found Denis's number online, and, eventually, I called him instead.

6.

Denis was a speech pathologist, it turned out. All these years I'd thought my father had said *palaeontologist*, so I was confused for a while. I'd even done some research and been side-tracked by the stories of a palaeontologist called Pierre Teilhard de Chardin, his time in China, his journeys in India and Egypt, and his obsession, paradoxical as it seemed, with the future of the universe. It didn't matter. None of this was related to Denis.

His secretary answered and put me through.

He had a gruff, deadpan manner. 'Are you working?' he asked. 'A wife? Kids?'

A few weeks later, I took the day off work — without telling Sarah — and drove out to visit him.

The speech-services building was opposite a big shopping centre in Ascot Vale, which was a suburb I'd never had much to do with. The roads were quiet that afternoon, and, coming down Dawson Street,

I had time to slow, although I don't know why I did, to glimpse the racecourse as I passed, which seemed luminous there in its patience, with its empty grandstands and its incongruous, manicured hedges in flower. The air was warm — it was almost spring, although in my own life it seemed as if everything was coming to an end. Afterwards, on the way back home, a mist of grey rain came down over the suburbs, and the light above the racetrack turned glassy. I pulled over and got out near the ambulance gate to walk the perimeter. In one spot, the chain-link fence had been ripped away from the ground, and, without thinking, I pulled it aside and snuck into the stadium. Then I made my way down the embankment, jumped a wooden barrier, and walked out onto the fresh, green turf.

'Your father and I were the larrikins,' Denis had told me when I called to ask if I could come see him. 'We had a lot of fun.' He wasn't having a lot of fun when he opened the door that day, though. He had a toothache and had recently broken his back, or so he claimed, lifting an old television out onto the nature strip.

'I'm still here, mate,' he said, when I asked how he was. I followed his painful shuffle down the hallway and into a bare consultation room, where we sat facing one another across an empty desk, across the two decades since we'd last had a conversation.

I didn't remember the last time I'd seen Denis, but I knew, more or less as a fact, that our last conversation had been about boxing. When I was a teenager, I often went with my father to watch the boxing on television at Denis's place, although my mother always pleaded with me not to. There were usually four or five other men and two women at these events, Denis's second wife, Conchitina, and another woman, called Ophelia. I remember Ophelia in particular, because of the way she screamed at the television in an alarming high-pitched voice. 'Fucking kill him!' she would scream, and a tiny pug would yap in agreement from the kitchen. That enduring cry throws into relief, now, the quietness of the men. The women were loud, funny, irreverent, violent. They bustled in and out of the room, chatting, laughing, carrying food, paying only intermittent attention to the fight. The men on the other hand barely moved, united by an aura of nervousness and respect. They made soft exclamations and swallowed their own grunts. They flinched noticeably. It was as if, in some not-too-distant reality, it was they themselves who were taking the blows. Beside me on the couch, my father would sway to avoid a punch thrown by the image of a boxer on the television, and our arms would touch.

Denis himself had become a half-decent amateur boxer in the early seventies, after his daughter, who was a baby at the time, died in her sleep. Boxing had seemed as good a response to this as anything else, and he was a wily, unpredictable, dirty fighter, who also had the advantage of being able to endure colossal amounts of physical punishment. According to my father, there had even been some talk of going pro, but that had been silenced for good the night he fought Alex 'The Janitor' Stavros. He retired as soon as he regained consciousness and was hospitalised for weeks after the fight. By this stage, his marriage had collapsed, or was on the brink of collapsing. I didn't feel much like pressing him on the details. Most of this I had gleaned over the years without paying too much attention. The rest Denis filled in for me as I sat considering the room around us. In a different world, I imagined, the walls might have been covered with children's drawings or family photographs.

Denis met my father in 1972, he told me, through a bloke he'd met in hospital called Barry, who knew a barmaid called Astra, who worked in a pub in St Kilda, where they all used to drink.

'And Astra,' Denis said, 'was your father's girlfriend.'

Back then Melbourne was just a weird little country town, none of this trendy stuff, Denis explained, and at night you could have fired a gun in any direction without having to worry about hitting someone. This was around the time that my dad bought the house in Byron Street, by accident, as it happened, at an auction into which he'd stumbled one afternoon, 'half pissed and stoned and everything else', according to Denis, after winning a significant sum of money on a horse called Transformer. This was during the period of his life when he was also claiming a disability pension from the Premier's Department.

'You know all this stuff, right?' Denis asked.

'Sort of,' I said. Which was sort of true. I'd heard the name Astra. I'd heard about my father's disability pension — the word *malingerer* stuck in my mind — but it was just a detail in a story I had never bothered to care about.

'Vince would ring me up,' Denis said, 'and he'd be like "Argh, I'm going for a drink", by which he meant he had to convince the doctor that he was a bit — *you know*.' Denis's eyes boggled.

'Crazy?'

'Unfit for work,' Denis said. 'Exactly. So he'd stay awake and drink for a few days and go to his appointment, shaking like a dog shitting razor blades, and then he'd tell the shrink, "If anyone sends *me* back to work they better watch their backs and their wife and their kids", and stuff like this.'

He laughed, and his laughter became a coughing fit.

'But you know,' he said, when he had recovered, 'I think there *were* some real issues with your father. Because he'd tried to neck himself already. He took some sleeping tablets and drank a couple of bottles of scotch. You know all this.'

'No.' I shook my head. I didn't. This was news to me.

Denis shrugged. 'Someone must have found him the next day with the blood supply cut off to his leg, which is why he had that dropped-foot all his life. His foot would catch on something and he'd be like: "Get that fucking thing outta the way!"'

This was something else I'd never realised. My father *was* always tripping over things and yelling at us, but I'd never known about this injury or the fact that he'd acquired it while trying to kill himself.

There was another thing Denis reminded me of. In 1991, he and my father went to America together, just the two of them — a strangely intimate experience, all things considered — to see Jeff Fenech fight Azumah Nelson in the open-air carpark of the Mirage Hotel in Las Vegas.

I remembered that trip. My father had called us from his hotel room, to tell us what had happened. After twelve rounds, the fight had been declared a draw. It was unbelievable, my father said. He sounded drunk but not unhappy. 'What time is it over there?' he kept asking. Then Tara told him something irrelevant, and finally my mother took the phone again, said something I don't remember, and hung up before I got a chance to say goodbye.

'It was a travesty,' Denis said. 'Fenech won convincingly. It was called the worst decision of the year or something like that.'

Days later, still hungover, still heartbroken, Denis and my father stood beside each other and looked down into the Grand Canyon. For some reason, *this* was what my father had wanted to see above all else, my mother told me later, when he grew tired of all those bars and buffet breakfasts and Black Russians. And so I imagined him standing there, euphoric, at the edge of that cliff at last. Unable to resist, he dips his hand into his pocket and flicks a coin up and out into the gullet of the great chasm. Denis was talking about something else by that stage, but I was imagining this: an American coin, as if from the movies, turning in slow motion above the Grand Canyon. My father, a gambler, a vandal, measuring infinity with a dumb gesture of defiance. *Heads or tails*, he says to Denis.

On the way home that day, as I've said, the rain came down. I ducked through the hole in the fence, jumped the barrier, and stepped out onto the racetrack where the fresh grass was glistening. This was Moonee Valley, I realised, a place I'd heard racing commentators referring to from pub televisions ever since I was a kid. The name had always evoked an image of jagged white mountains, like an aged black-and-white photo I must have seen somewhere. I took a deep breath and tried not to think about what would happen if somebody stopped me. I walked and walked, expecting at any moment to hear the voice of a security guard. But nothing happened; just faint grey rain like a thickening of the air and crows *arking* among the pines in the no-man's-land that lay in the middle of the track. Eventually, I stopped thinking. The smell of earth and grass. In front of the stadium, on the far side, I could see figures in fluorescent jackets, but I had become invisible to them — I had slipped out of the world altogether. And even when I entered the straight, close enough to see their faces, and jumped the fence again, and headed out towards the members' carpark, they continued to ignore me. They were big guys, with red faces and grey goatees, but I guess it wasn't their job to give a shit.

7.

Most nights after that, I stayed up watching boxing videos on YouTube until I fell asleep and dropped the phone into my lap. Then Sylvie would cry out, and I would wake and run to settle her with the pressure of my hand on her chest and a few renditions of 'Silent Night' or the ABC. When it worked, it was like a superpower, and then I would go back to the couch, and pick up where I had left off, watching men punch each other in the head.

The Fenech/Nelson rematch took place the year after their first fight, on 2 March 1992, at Princes Park, in Melbourne. Denis and my dad were there for that as well. I remembered seeing them that night on the Channel 7 news, walking through the crowd together, the image of my father made fantastic by television.

You can watch *Fenech v Nelson II* easily enough now on YouTube, but the footage I remember watching is grainier and even harder to make out. Most of the boxing I saw as a kid was like that: lurid, alarming, mesmerising footage, obscured by time and fading technology, which my dad had taped and retaped onto VHS cassettes and then marked carefully (*Fenech v Payakaroon, Tyson v Botha, Fenech v Shingaki II*), and which he kept at the top of the bookshelf beside the whiskey. Two conjoined names signifying a supernatural occasion.

Fenech v Nelson II was somehow different, and my father seemed to return to it on nights when he couldn't sleep, as if it held some mystery he was trying to unravel. I remember watching him once, as I stood unseen on the brass carpet plate that marked a border between the kitchen and the back room. After my bedtime that back room became a forbidden zone; dark, green-ish, often smoky. I remember my father's face in the glow of the fight, and the way he moved gently with the punches as the luck drained away from Jeff Fenech's life.

They had both felt that something wasn't right that day, Denis told me. Fenech had looked slow from the beginning; he'd forgotten to make the sign of the cross before the bell and then, in the first round, he'd stepped into an unspectacular overhand right, like a man who had woken up with a hangover and walked straight into a door. Fenech kept fighting, of course — he didn't know how to give up — and he took the seventh convincingly, but in the eighth, a round spent locked in what looked like a titanic thumb-wrestle — both fighters pounding away with their heads resting on each other's shoulders — Nelson finally produced an opening and rocked Fenech with a left hook, then another, and then a right that felled him sideways. Fenech got up, but he had acquired an expression of bewildered innocence. The best part of him, the part that made sense of all the rest, was dying up there. With his back to the ropes, he stood for his execution.

One night I found an online documentary about Jeff Fenech. He was a man who fluctuated between moods of tremendous goodwill and foolish anger. The lessons that he kept claiming to have learnt never seemed to stay learnt for long. Many years after his retirement, he would be attacked on the street by four men. They smashed a bottle into his face. Some time later, gangsters shot up his family house. Later still, he was caught shoplifting watches on the Gold Coast. At the age of forty-three, he tried to redeem his loss to Nelson in a final rematch, but they were both old men by this stage. Nelson was forty-nine at least (no one knew exactly), and though Fenech won on points, it was too late: the stakes were too low, and nothing was really redeemed.

'Come look at this,' I said to Sarah.

Jeff Fenech was on the screen. He was in Princes Park, fighting for his life. My father was there, too, somewhere in the crowd, twenty-five rows from the front. Sooner or later, I'd spot him.

'You know, you actually live with two real people,' Sarah said.

I looked up at her tired face, which was shining with moisturiser. 'What?'

She shook her head. 'I'm going to sleep.'

But we both knew she wouldn't sleep. And anyway, what boxing story ends happily?

8.

'Maybe instead of watching boxing videos on YouTube you could figure out how to put a child to sleep,' Sarah suggested one day. There were other things she suggested, too. One evening, I heard her laughing in the kitchen. But when I came in from the backyard, she wasn't laughing. She was standing against the fridge, crying.

I tried to touch her, but she slapped my hand away. 'We're not working,' she said at last. 'There's no family if there's no us, and there's no *us*.'

'I don't know what you're talking about,' I said, although I guess I did.

'If this is the price,' she said — our distance from one another, my practical assistance, which felt empty to her, though I myself felt utterly drained by it, completely exhausted, as if I were treading water at the very limit of myself — 'If this is the price, then I wish we'd never done it.'

'What do you want to do?' I asked.

'Why don't *you* figure something out for once?' she yelled.

But her rage was incoherent to me. It seemed to come from another world. It was not unlike my father's, in that regard. She wanted to destroy everything. I felt something icy snap shut: my own contempt, like a steel roller-door, slamming down between us.

We argued until Sylvie woke again, and then Sarah ran to her, and I went out into the darkness and watered the garden, furiously pounding the fragile vegetables into the dirt. Overhead a few dull stars flickered above the suburbs, above the Hills hoist and the neighbour's cable-television satellite dish.

The next day, I called my dad's old friend Charlie.

'You wanna know why your daddy topped himself, is that it?' Charlie asked.

'Thanks,' I said. 'Nice. Yeah, I guess.'

'Go,' Sarah said, with what seemed like a flourish of generosity. 'I hope it does you some good.'

9.

The thing I thought about when I thought about Charlie was a name — *Emerald City* — and a story that went with it. I remembered my father telling this story at the dinner table, more than once, throwing his arms out, grinning, holding back the crucial details like good cards, which he then laid down dramatically before us.

Yeah, yeah, I would think, and Tara would roll her eyes. The past was a foreign country, and who cared what they did there.

I rang Tara from the train station in Brisbane.

'What do you remember about Charlie?' I asked her.

Tara lived in Adelaide now. She had found her way. She was happy, I think. She had three dogs, a nice husband called Gus, and twins — tiny, freakishly identical girls with wild black hair. Sometimes they shook their heads at the same time and scared the hell out of me.

Tara remembered almost nothing about Charlie, she said, and nothing at all about Emerald City. Just photos, and Charlie's accent, and going to his house once, or what she supposed was his house, in the mountains somewhere, or the hills.

'That was a weird day,' she said.

'When did this happen?'

'I don't know,' she said, 'but I remember turning up and there was a forest with, I don't know, like old bits of rides, from a fairground or something, scattered in the trees. It was like another planet.'

'Wait, was I there?'

'Yeah, you were there. I think you were there.'

'I don't think I was there,' I said.

'Wait, was *I* there?' she laughed.

'And what happened?'

'I don't know,' she said. 'I can't remember, but it was like alchemy, and Nietzsche and the reformation.' She couldn't stop laughing. 'I don't know, maybe it was a dream? No, it wasn't a dream. I don't know. The French Revolution. That was it. Something historical like that, anyway.'

She also remembered Charlie's formidable presence, which was what I remembered, too. He was a big, loud, articulate, intimidating Irishman, whose bald, battle-scarred head, or so it seemed to me when I was small, almost touched the ceiling in our back room in Byron Street. In my memory, Charlie had to stoop simply to stand there, but this was a falsification of mine, I realised, since it was Charlie, together with my father, who actually built that room, in the mid-seventies. Beginning at about eight in the morning, when Charlie arrived, this building process had involved an enormous amount of cask wine, which he and my father continued to drink from Vegemite jars until well into the evening, by which point, of course, they would have been too drunk to build anything.

But even these details were not something I knew before I arrived.

I knew only that Charlie was my father's friend, that he had been an alcoholic, a history teacher, and a member, for a few years, of a radical commune called 'Emerald City' in far northern New South Wales. Also, that he had a daughter called Neve, who was a few years older than me, and with who I rode the ghost train at Luna Park one afternoon when we were children. Beside her I became very brave, and together we made that trip thirteen times in a row, which was a record, I believe.

It was nearly midnight, but Charlie was waiting when I stepped onto the platform. He nodded at me. He was still very tall, though he looked emaciated now. We hadn't seen each other for nearly twenty years, just once since my father's funeral, but he did not make a fuss about this. He seemed to be guarding himself against sentimentality, as if he expected his generosity to be abused. Taking one of my bags without comment, he led me into the tiny gravel carpark behind the station. I looked around, trying to understand where I was. I saw lights among the palm trees, and a distant orange glow, where the cane fields were on fire. Then we drove, with the windows down, through thick, rushing darkness.

'How's your mother?' Charlie yelled above the sound of the wind.

I slept badly that night in Charlie's spare room and woke, thinking that Sylvie was crying nearby. I checked my phone. Seven missed calls from Sarah. No messages. It was 4am. When I called, no one answered. I got up and walked out into the silent kitchen. The door to

Charlie's room was ajar, and I could see his wife, Lucy, sleeping beside him with her face turned towards me and her mouth open. Weird to see someone sleeping before you've even met them. I drank a glass of water and opened the fridge, which was filled with small plastic bottles of medicine, but almost no food.

When I woke again, it was late, a warm winter Queensland morning, and I could hear voices in the kitchen. Lucy smiled when I came out and we shook hands. Then she handed me my breakfast utensils one by one, while Charlie paced back and forth between the kitchen and the computer in the next room. The Brexit vote was happening. He was hoping for anarchy.

'I'll leave you guys to it,' Lucy said sceptically, when I'd finished my breakfast. She'd never met my father. I was a messenger from an unpleasant world that had nothing to do with her. Charlie was Lucy's third husband. She was Charlie's fifth wife. His first, second, and fourth wives were far away, and didn't speak to him anymore. His third wife, Rochelle, lived in an aged-care facility across the road. He went and read to her every so often. Rochelle had Alzheimer's and didn't talk to him either, because she didn't know who he was. This was probably for the best, Charlie admitted. 'I don't think I was very good company, while we were married. I certainly didn't try very hard not to be an alcoholic.'

Of course, Charlie didn't know why my father had killed himself. He didn't know why he was so angry. He didn't remember him being angry at all. He'd loved my father.

'Vincent was the only real friend I ever had,' Charlie told me. 'But he was a mystery to me. It was a mystery how we ever got to be friends in the first place. Then again, I've got such disturbing ideas about myself, I've never understood why *anyone* would want to be my friend.'

Which was why he lived out here among the rednecks, he explained, where nobody wanted anything to do with him.

'You're my first visitor in I don't know how long.'

'What about your daughter?' I asked. 'Does she count?'

'Neve doesn't come,' he said. 'She lives in London with her stockbroker. She goes skiing in Switzerland instead of coming to see me. But you've got a kid, don't you? Your mother said something about that, I remember. A long time ago. Did it happen?'

'It did,' I said. 'It happened. She's two.'

'Good to hear it,' he said. 'Just don't expect her to come visit you in twenty-five years.'

Charlie was out on parole, he told me, when he and my father first met. This was back in the early seventies. My father was a parole officer at the time, and, on certain days, Charlie said, he would take a crew of eight or so minor criminals out into the community to mow people's lawns, or paint church halls, or 'weed out the blackberries in some little old lady's overgrown back garden'. At lunchtime, according to Charlie, they'd sit around smoking cigarettes and telling lies about their hard lives. Then, most days, they would knock off early and go play pool at the pub. This was forbidden, but it was the seventies, so it didn't seem like there was much that was *strictly* forbidden, and anyway, Charlie said, everyone else in the public service was drunk by lunchtime.

'Your daddy was paid to keep an eye on me,' Charlie said, 'but really, it could just as easily have been the other way round.'

It was a job my father had loved, apparently, and which lasted until a new boss was appointed who'd had other ideas. There was an altercation, and my father, who had always felt persecuted, and who suffered from nightmares, drove around to his new boss's house and unscrewed the front door.

'So that was the end of that job,' Charlie laughed. 'He put the door in the back of the ute and drove away.'

'And what about Emerald City?' I asked. This was what I really wanted to know about. The commune.

'Emerald City,' Charlie said, stretching out his enormous legs and leaning back in his chair. 'Those were the fucking days, weren't they?'

'Were they?'

'No,' he laughed. 'Fuck no. Sooner I forget all about that fucking place, the happier I'll be.'

It was Sally, wife number one, Charlie said, who first heard about Emerald City. This would have been the end of 1975, the start of 1976. Charlie was drinking a lot and painting big abstract expressionist paintings, and meanwhile his marriage was dying. That's when Sally came home with the idea, Charlie said. Something had to change. Also, Sally was pregnant. They needed a fresh start.

'We thought maybe we should drink goat's milk and eat yucky food every day and be free from the structures of society.'

So they packed the car, and sold everything that didn't fit.

When they first arrived, it was barely a dozen people. Gradually, others began to arrive — friends of friends, families, actors, musicians, professors of sociology, then just some pretty shifty types of people, criminals basically, Charlie said. There was a brief reference that corroborated this description in Bob Mollard's *Utopian Dreaming*, an old sun-damaged green pamphlet, which Charlie pulled down from the bookshelf for me. Then the whole place fell apart in the early eighties, and was bulldozed by the locals.

While it worked — and, in a kind of way, it seemed to, for a few years — people worked together with their hands, with axes and chainsaws, with paintbrushes and hammers and needles and thread. Neve was born. Sally yarned, and set up an ill-fated garment-making cooperative, Charlie told me, while he scrounged for materials and stole things. He tore apart old cars and washing machines and put them back together again as geodesic domes.

'Vincent came and helped with some of that stuff,' Charlie said, and he claimed to have a photo of my father standing on the roof of one of those domes. He'd try and dig it out for me, he promised. 'Those fucking domes always leaked, though,' he laughed, and in the end, they gave up on the domes.

It was raining the last time my father went up to Emerald City. Charlie remembered this, he said, because Vincent had just got back from somewhere or other and it was nice to see him. Also, Charlie had just blown a hole in his own roof with a rifle. This was the story I remembered. The rifle had been a birthday gift, a few years earlier. A Lee-Enfield .303. My father had given it to him.

It must have been in 1977, Charlie said, because Elvis was dead and 'someone had been playing "Burning Love" on repeat for three fucking days', during which time it hadn't stopped raining. The rifle, which Charlie had been using to shoot kangaroos, had just gone off. Who knows how? Charlie was too drunk to understand. The bullet had passed through the narrow gap between Sally and their two-year-old daughter, Neve, and blown a hole in the roof. Now the roof was leaking again.

When he arrived, later that afternoon, my father must have thought: *Fantastic, here's something for me to fix.*

Sally, I guessed, thought something different.

Charlie thought: *Fuck. Fuck.*

He sat for a long time with his head in his hands, in relief, in horror, he told me. But also, in despair, because he knew that somehow, it wasn't an accident. A part of him must have wanted to shoot his way out of there. This part of him thought: *I have escaped into a trap.* The wife. The kid. The nagging.

'This wasn't anarchism,' he said. 'This was domestic fucking servitude. The rain, and the wet washing, and the mud. The smell of things bloody rotting. *Utopia, my arse,*' he laughed.

Some time passed. Charlie went out and threw the shotgun down a well, he said. Then he staggered back through the mud, a flagon of wine in his hand and his kaftan clinging to his body. He needed to get out of there. He'd be doing Sally a favour, although it wouldn't be the first time he'd done her a favour by running away, he told me. At some point the remorse always kicked in, and then he had to beg her to take him back again. He knew all these things, but none of them seemed to be a very powerful thought in that moment. *I'll drive west*, he remembered thinking. Or south. Not north in any case, not through Queensland, which was fascist territory in those days, under Bjelke-Petersen. He'd imagined the road unfurling in front of him, he said, and he'd started to feel pretty good. *A man who drinks is interplanetary*, somebody once wrote. *He moves through interstellar space.*

When Charlie looked up again, he saw two figures stomping towards him through the white day.

Who the fuck is this? he thought.

It was my father.

And somebody else.

'There was some other bloke came up with your dad,' Charlie told me.

'Who?'

Charlie closed his eyes.

'Handsome bloke,' he said at last. 'American.'

'Abbie?' I said.

Charlie shrugged. 'Maybe. But they were good mates. Him and your dad. I was jealous.'

Whoever he was, this man and my father helped Charlie back to his dome, apparently. The door was locked. They banged on the metal panels. But Sally wouldn't let them in.

'Fuck off, you fucking fuckwits,' she yelled.

'Alright, fair enough, geez.'

So they'd walked up the hill, and lit a fire beside Vincent's Monaro. The wood was wet, but they poured petrol over everything and chucked matches at it until the flames whooshed up. At some point others arrived, Charlie remembered — two girls and a bloke dressed like a clown, who was handing out bowls of mush. Then they all sat around the fire smoking joints, mesmerised by their own destinies.

'And what was my dad doing?' I wanted to know. 'What was he saying?'

I imagined him telling stories about his adventures in India. I imagined him spreading his arms wide. But what *were* his adventures?

He never mentioned them to me. I can almost see his mouth moving, but I can't hear anything.

Charlie didn't remember what his adventures were either. 'Nope,' he said. 'He kept all that stuff to himself.'

But later that night, while Charlie slept in the back of his car, Vincent and the American climbed down into the well to retrieve the rifle. If Charlie didn't want it, then Vincent would take it back. They stashed it under a blanket in the boot of the Monaro. That gun had once belonged to my grandfather. I knew this, because my father *had* told me that part of the story. Before he died, my father gave the gun to me.

The day after all this happened at Emerald City, Charlie said, Sally left for good. She took Neve to Sydney, where she stayed with her sister and eventually got a job as a librarian. Charlie stayed on in Emerald City for a while. Then he burnt all his paintings and left, he told me. He travelled around. He worked as a ditch digger and as a cook in the Adelaide Hills. He built fences. He was a courier. Then, in March 1978, he got a job driving a small truck, which he rolled, drunk, on the border of South Australia and Victoria, and managed to crawl out of alive. My father drove up and collected him from the hospital, and Charlie came down and slept on our couch in Byron Street for a few weeks. I'd seen photos of that, his neck in a brace. His broken leg. I was three months old at the time. Charlie held me in his arms and rocked me back and forth. Then he joined AA. Then he went back to university and studied to become a school teacher. He taught history and politics for many years, though what he really wanted was to teach philosophy. He seemed to recognise in Nietzsche's portrayal of Zarathustra an image of himself: a hermit breaking reluctantly from the tranquillity of the mountain cave in order to enlighten — and inevitably fail to enlighten — a herd of idiots.

'My relationship with your father never changed,' he told me. 'We didn't have a lot of contact, but it didn't matter. We never went our separate ways. It was a true friendship. I'd never had one of those before. I still hear the sound of his car coming round the corner sometimes.'

Charlie's voice had died down to a whisper by this point, a thin, whistly thread that finally trailed off altogether. His eyes were closed. It was late afternoon. Lucy was home now. We could hear her bustling around in the other room. My train to Brisbane would leave in a few hours. My family was waiting for me. My wife and child.

Charlie opened his eyes again. 'You look just like him,' he said. 'It's a wee bit fucking spooky, actually.'

Charlie never did find the photo of my father on the roof of the dome at Emerald City. He looked for it for a while, and then he must have forgotten all about it. Or perhaps it never existed to begin with.

Some months later, I sent Charlie an email despairing of Trump's recent election, and Charlie sent me a short email in return, excoriating my *limp liberal pieties*. He was celebrating the result as a step in the right direction. *Only a global catastrophe will reset the corrupt order of the world*, he wrote. We exchanged a few more emails in the following weeks, friendly notes about books or movies, and then one afternoon, he sent me a single line:

I've decided I want no further contact with you.

Charlie had loved my father. Maybe he was afraid he would start loving me, too. Or maybe it was something else. I wasn't my father; maybe *that* was the problem. Maybe I was just a disappointment to him.

10.

One night, a few weeks before he died, my father came home and woke me up. When I opened my eyes, he was swivelling around in the chair beside my bed, whistling. On his head he was wearing a tattered Johnnie Walker cap that I'd never seen before, and which didn't really suit him. It made him look older than he was. But he wasn't old. He was only forty-three. He was still a handsome man, although that's not what I thought at the time. I could smell him. He had a smell I wish I could smell again. Sweat and tobacco and motor oil and wood. His fingers often bled from the work he did. Sometimes it took him half an hour to wash the grease from his hands.

'Come have a drink,' he said, and he passed me a beer.

I grunted. I didn't really feel like drinking. I felt like being asleep. But I took the beer anyway, and I got up and followed him out through the dark house and into the backyard. My mother was asleep. Tara was asleep. The cats and the rabbits and the dog and the budgies were asleep. It must have been two or three in the morning, in January, because the Christmas tree was turning yellow, all the windows were open, and there were moths beating through the cobwebs to get to the light above the garage door. That's where we sat, beneath the moths, with our backs to the garage, smoking in silence. My father smoked very strong tobacco, which, for a while, I had tried to smoke, too, but we had never smoked together like this, even though he knew that I did smoke, because I had been sent home from school for doing it. My father was not angry about that. In fact, soon afterwards, he bought me a large amount of illegally grown, untaxed tobacco, as a reward. My mother was angry about *that*. 'If he's going to smoke, he's going to smoke,' my father told her, and this was the tobacco I was smoking that night. It came in a large plastic bag. And maybe there was a novelty about that scenario that I should have appreciated, smoking together at last, like adults, although the truth was that my father's presence irritated me. I suppose he was drunk, although that was not uncommon. What was worse was that he seemed to be waiting for a chance to confide in me. And then he began telling me a story about a woman he had lived with, before he'd met my mother, in this very house, he said, in the early seventies. The woman's name was Astra.

'Isn't that a type of car?' I said.

Actually, he said, sounding hurt, she was a remarkable woman. She was a tarot reader who had psychic dreams and who believed in UFOs. And one New Year's Eve, they had walked naked together along an empty beach in a lightning storm.

Oh, you've got to be kidding me, I thought. I did not want to hear this story. I did not care about some old lady called Astra.

11.

Now Astra was walking towards me, barefoot down the dirt driveway. She was dressed in a long black dress, and she had a shaved head, and big gold earrings that swung back and forth. We shook hands.

'Yeah,' she said softly, drawing out the word and nodding as she stepped back to examine me. She had a serious face, and pale grey eyes like foggy crystal balls. Then she stepped forward again and hugged me. She smelt of earth or weed or mushrooms or unpasteurised milk, something like that — a dense, living, animal smell. I could feel her bones.

Astra lived an hour out of Mullumbimby, on land strewn with rotting trees. To get there from the main road you had to follow a series of winding dirt tracks, cross two small bridges, and then take the third left past a hidden encampment of derelict cars, goats, and half-built sheds reinforced with blue plastic tarpaulins. Further along this road there was a cream-brick farmhouse, set back among straight rows of palm trees, with a rectangular arena of dirty sand out the front. This was Astra's closest neighbour. From where we stood now, we could see a woman on a horse taking very small steps. Some sort of dressage champion, apparently.

'Just ignore her,' Astra said. 'She's a fucking bitch.'

Inside, the house was neat, dark, loosely bohemian. We sat at the kitchen table, among cactuses and plants, and brass statues of Hindu gods who were bathing in the blood of demon decapitation. It was five in the afternoon. Astra had told me to come for dinner and had offered me the spare bedroom, which I had accepted.

'So,' she said, folding her hands in her lap. We looked at each other in silence for a moment. In the dimness, it was as if we'd just stepped off the street into a cinema. The movie had already started, but we didn't know what it was about yet.

I had found Astra on Facebook a month earlier, and we had written back and forth trying to arrange a time to meet. I knew that she had been a barmaid back when that was still the term, in a pub off Punt Road, in the late 1960s. Denis had told me that. I knew that she had been a tarot reader and a student counsellor, because my father had said so, and that she was an Integrated Clinical Hypnotherapist now — I'd seen her website — and a member of the Australian and New Zealand Society of Jungian Analysts. From Facebook I knew that she had signed petitions against the government's treatment of asylum seekers and had attended, or at least planned to attend, a number of rallies for climate justice and marriage equality in the last year. I'd seen her holiday photos from Japan and knew that she had donated to a fund to help rebuild a Buddhist shrine that had been damaged by the tsunami in 2011. I knew that she grew her own vegetables, and made kombucha and bread and jewellery. I knew (again from Facebook) that she had a partner called Tess, who was also a therapist of some sort, and that she had at least two grown children, a daughter called Indra, who was a yoga teacher in San Francisco (I'd seen Indra's Instagram account), and a son called Rhett (Facebook), who was a connoisseur of extremely violent computer games and a supporter, it seemed, of Donald Trump. Astra must have been about sixty-four years old, I calculated, because she'd been thirteen in 1966, when three UFOs had come down and hovered above the sports oval, before lifting off again and disappearing into the area of woodland that lay behind her school. This was in the Melbourne suburb of Westall, near Clayton, where she had grown up. I remembered my father telling me this story in the backyard that night. I remembered the way his eyes grew watery, and his nostrils flared, as he tried to find the simple words to describe his affection for this woman. Words I had long forgotten, though I thought I could remember the look on his face: excited, credulous, idiotic. *What am I supposed to do with this story?* I remember thinking. But when I looked into it years later, as I was preparing to meet Astra, I found a documentary on YouTube about the incident. It was a real thing. There were more than two hundred witnesses.

'Did you see it?' I asked.

'See what?'

'The documentary?'

'Oh,' Astra said. 'Is that what you're here for?' She leant back in her chair, assessing me.

'No,' I said. 'Not really. It was just something I remembered Dad mentioning. The UFOs, I mean.'

'Yeah,' she said, extending the word again so that it implied not simply affirmation but also a kind of open-ended, vague thoughtfulness. She had the slow, comforting, soporific inflection of many old hippies. 'Yeah,' she said again, she'd seen the documentary. Some guy had called her and they'd talked, although she hadn't wanted to appear onscreen or be associated with it in any way. The whole UFO world, we agreed, could get pretty wacky. Nevertheless, she claimed, the memory of the incident was clearer to her than almost anything else that had happened in her childhood.

She had been among a group of kids who ran and jumped the wire fence and arrived at a clearing in the pine trees. The disc hovered in front of her, a few feet above the ground. From where she stood, five or six metres away, she said, it seemed as big as a car. She could feel the heat coming off it. It was silver. It hummed softly. There were lights along the bottom that she saw as it lifted and tilted away. A girl nearby was screaming. Another girl was lying in the grass where she had fainted. The disc rose slowly, then shot up into the sky and vanished almost instantly. Half an hour later, according to the documentary, the army arrived, although the army denies this. The girl who had fainted — Tania — never came back to school, and when Astra dropped by her house a few days later, to see if she was alright, her family were gone. A woman was living there, Astra said, who claimed to know nothing about the previous occupants. Astra never saw Tania again, she told me, but later she heard rumours that Tania was in Brisbane and had become a nun. She had taken a vow of silence, or, at least, she refused to speak when two of her old classmates turned up at the door of the convent. She had looked at them in terror, apparently, and turned away.

'It all seems pretty crazy now,' Astra admitted. 'But yeah.' She shrugged.

Astra had met my father back in 1972, she told me, when they were both working as volunteers for a community organisation called 'The Workshop', a kind of anarchist collective that operated out of a little house in Prahran. I'd heard stories about it from my father, though I'd never bothered to connect them together into something that seemed like real life. Weeks later, at the State Library in Melbourne, I found copies of the little magazine they'd put out — *The Worker* — a name that was somewhat ironic, Astra pointed out, since everyone involved with it was on the dole. But they *did* work, it seemed to me, in their own way. They had a helpline and an information referral service where they dispensed advice about abortions and tenancy disputes and bad trips. They organised crash pads for people who found themselves with nowhere to sleep and offered a free legal service. At some point, they started a food co-op and began helping draft dodgers. Once, Astra said, they even managed to break someone out of the Royal Park Psychiatric Hospital, though she'd had nothing to do with that personally.

'Was Dad involved?' I asked.

She didn't know.

Astra and my father had worked the telephones together every Tuesday night, comforting the lonely and trying to talk people out of killing themselves, even though, as Astra admitted, 'We were just kids. We had no proper training, and really, what did we know about anything.' While the phones were silent, it was just the two of them. They had hours to themselves. Astra moved into Dad's place in Byron Street sometime in 1973.

'Vince and I had a scene together for a while,' she said, opening the fridge door and squinting into the light.

We were drinking mid-strength Asahi, but we'd already had quite a few. She placed two fresh bottles on the table between us, and then sat down again and began flicking back and forth through her diary, which she'd gone to the trouble of digging out for the occasion. She was trying to jog her memory. Her diary from those years had dates, names, events, but not much more than that.

'May 19, 1974,' she said. 'Labor re-elected.'

'August 1974: party for Peter Moksin,' she said. 'But I don't remember who Peter Moksin was.'

'April 14, 1974. Party for Mike's film at Byron Street.'

'Who was Mike?' I asked.

'He was a filmmaker, who hung around with Vince for a while,' she said. 'He was quite attractive. I had a fling with him, actually. Which caused all sorts of trouble.'

'While you were with Dad?'

She shrugged.

The pages kept turning.

'Ron,' she said. 'Manic,' she said. 'Steve,' she said. Names I didn't recognise, and which had something to do with a transcendental meditation group that used to meet up in the spare bedroom. Later it evolved into a pretty heavy political situation, Astra explained. Or maybe it was the other way round, the heavy politics turning inward. She couldn't remember.

'That big room just off the front door,' she said. 'Everyone was always in there humming or doing whatever.'

'That was my sister's bedroom.'

'That was a lot of people's bedroom,' she said, turning another page. 'But when you think about the number of people who passed through Byron Street, one way or another, you do sort of wonder how that worked. It was a pretty hectic scene.'

How *did* it work? I wanted to know. What did my father think about all these people coming and going? It was disconcerting to imagine him as a landlord, if that's what he was, or as some kind of still centre, which is what he seemed to me in this account, a strangely absent figure, like a spectre that allowed these situations, these people, to simply move around him.

'I didn't think of him like that,' Astra said. 'You know, everyone really liked your dad. Is that what you want to hear?'

'No,' I said. I was pretty sure that wasn't what I wanted to hear. I thought of my father, when I did think of him, in quick bursts, like fireworks: brilliant, fading, repetitive memories that were incapable of becoming anything else. I tried to explain this to her. I wanted to find out something I didn't know.

'I'd much rather you told me something terrible,' I said.

'Be careful what you wish for.'

'Really?'

'I don't know.'

'Was he angry with you, or was it just with us?' I asked.

'That's not my memory,' she said, clearing her throat. 'My overwhelming memory, actually, was just fear. For him, I mean. That he'd hurt himself.'

'Drinking?'

'Drinking. Driving. That's a start.'

'Why was he such a bad driver?'

'I've got no idea. But I guess he always had a kind of death wish, didn't he?'

'What else do you remember?'

She shook her head. 'Not much,' she said. She'd met my grandparents once. She knew that my father's relationship with them wasn't good. He had an older brother, my uncle, who was dead now, too, and who had worked on a fishing trawler in Canada for a while. 'Or was it an oil rig?' she asked.

But I didn't know.

'His brother used to call up every Christmas Eve,' Astra said, 'very drunk.'

Vincent had gotten his tattoos at twelve, she told me, 'but you probably know about that.'

I knew about the tattoos. I didn't know that he had been expelled at the age of fifteen for throwing a table out a window, or that he had never finished high school, or that he was once arrested for stealing a car, but never charged. Nor did I know that his parents sent him away when he was six or seven years old, to live, for a few months, with a man called Mr Sugar.

'Who was Mr Sugar?' I asked.

'Vince never mentioned him?'

'No.'

'I think he was just a pretty unpleasant, abusive kind of person,' Astra said. But she couldn't tell me much more than that.

The last time she spoke to my father, she told me, was on the telephone. 'I remember he called me from some little town,' Astra said. 'I suppose he was on acid, or at least he sounded like he was. And then he must have run out of coins. That would have been 1976. Just before he went overseas.'

'To India?'

'I think so. We lost touch.'

She also remembered that he had lots of guns.

'What was it with all those guns?' I asked.

'Yeah,' she said softly. 'I couldn't say. But I guess, if you own lots of guns, you probably feel like you need to protect yourself from something.'

We sat in silence again while Astra massaged the gold rings on her fingers. Maybe she had been beautiful once, I thought — she had certainly been young — and I tried to see it, but I saw something hard instead, like a black stone at the bottom of an ornamental pond.

While we had been sitting there, three boys had drifted through the house and disappeared around the corner of the balcony. They were shy, neat men in their late twenties, at a guess, who belonged somehow, I assumed, to Tess, because Astra ignored them. As it turned out, they were friends of Rhett, the Trump-kid I'd seen on Facebook, who was, in fact, Tess's son, not Astra's, and who was twenty-seven years old and still lived at home, in a bungalow around the back. Which was where he was now, Astra explained, playing a Vietnam War game called *Rising Storm 2*.

'It's very realistic,' she said.

Now that I thought about it, I realised I could hear the faint sound of explosions and screaming, mingling with the Balinese water feature and the shrill, flicking call of an unknown bird somewhere in the palm trees. Tess was not at home at the moment, and I tried to clarify whether this meant today, or ever, but Astra stood up, stretching her bangled wrists above her head, and excused herself.

The house had grown dark by this stage, and, while Astra was in the bathroom, I sat at the table alone, looking around at the room. I was trying to work how to raise the topic of Astra's psychic powers. Was that really what my father had said? What had she foreseen? Faced with the reality of this woman now, that story seemed fairly dubious.

From the bathroom, I heard the toilet flush. But Astra didn't return. I looked again at the room around me and seemed to discern an aura of loneliness and dishevelment that I hadn't detected earlier, a chaos that had been hurriedly smoothed flat in the hours or minutes before I arrived. Suddenly, I knew that Tess wasn't coming back, that she didn't live here anymore.

When Astra finally emerged, she went into the kitchen and stood with her back to the fridge. She looked different, somehow, but I couldn't have said why.

'What was I saying?' she asked.

I looked at my notes. The word 'Mike' was underlined three times.

'Someone called Mike?'

'Was I?' She seemed confused. 'Yeah. Okay. I don't know what happened to him, though I guess I could probably find out.'

She was still for a while but then she turned to face the window and placed her palms down on the stone bench. I waited. A moth fizzed off my head like a rubber band.

'I have this vision, actually,' she said at last. 'I'm on the freeway with your dad. The Tullamarine freeway. It's late at night. He's doing wheelies. Burnouts, whatever they're called, going round and round.'

'Donuts?' I said. 'What year would this have been?'

'I remember all that smoke,' she continued. 'I'm surprised I'm still here.' She closed her eyes. 'Mike was there, too,' she said. Then she opened her eyes again, although she remained where she was, as if afraid to move. 'I can see him standing there as we go round,' she said.

'Your dad's driving, I've got my head out the window. I'm screaming. And Mike's standing on the concrete embankment in the middle of the highway. He must have been filming it. He was a filmmaker. Did I say that?'

Just then there was a noise, and we both turned towards the doorway and saw a person who was almost certainly Tess walk into the room. She was a short, muscular woman, in her sixties, I assumed, and she was still wearing a bike helmet with a flashing red light.

There was a moment's pause before I spoke to introduce myself, as if the very atoms of the room were rearranging themselves, settling into a new configuration. Something ebbed away. Just a few moments earlier, as far as I was concerned, Tess had been as good as dead.

'That's right,' Tess said, extending her hand. 'I forgot you were coming.'

She walked to the sink and filled a glass with water from the tap. The light on her helmet made the dark room throb like an emergency.

'We were just talking about the seventies,' Astra said. 'And Mike,' she added, as if the name itself was a kind of provocation.

'Uh huh,' said Tess, drinking. She put the glass on the edge of the bench. 'Mike who?'

'Mike what's-his-face,' said Astra, coming back to the table and slumping down with one leg crossed beneath her. It was a forced display of nonchalance. If saying Mike's name had been a challenge, she seemed to have backed down already. She closed the diary on the table and picked up her phone instead. 'Mike you-know,' she said, flicking at the screen.

'Mike Tadic?'

'Yeah.'

'With the screwdriver?'

'Yeah.'

'Did you know Mike?' I asked Tess. 'What's this about a screwdriver?'

'Old friend of Astra's,' Tess said, removing her helmet finally and switching off the light. 'Tried to kill himself by running into a tree with a screwdriver pointed at his heart. That's right, isn't it?'

Astra nodded without looking up.

'Then he tried to set himself on fire,' Tess said. "Have you eaten?'

We hadn't. Astra had forgotten all about dinner.

'Shit,' she said. 'I'm sorry,' though she remained where she was, slumped across the table now, like a teenager in mock exhaustion. I waited for Tess to say something else about Mike, or dinner. Instead, she turned and disappeared down the hallway. Astra smiled, but in her eyes, something seemed to have burnt out.

I had a dream that night, a variation on a recurring theme, in which I cornered a dying man. *Do you remember my father?* I asked him, and in my hand I had a hammer with which I bludgeoned his head. I woke and lay in darkness, sensing the presence of other dreams slipping away behind this one. It was three-thirty in the morning. Someone was snoring in the next room. Finally, I got up and went out quietly through the side door. Beyond the house, a grass clearing the size of two or three sports fields stretched away towards a wall of black mountain. I walked through the long grass and stood looking up. The sky was pale with galaxies. All around, the sound of crickets and frogs and whatever else was out there, living in the dirt and the trees.

'Hi,' said a voice.

I spun around. Astra was sitting in a chair about ten metres away, almost invisible in the dark. A match flared up.

'Fuck,' I said. 'Sorry, I didn't mean …'

'It's fine,' she said, exhaling smoke towards the sky. 'This is what I do if I can't sleep.' She coughed. 'We need to cut this grass.'

We were quiet for a while.

'It's my birthday today,' she said at last.

'Happy birthday,' I said.

She tried to smile. I saw her teeth. 'Anyway,' she said, 'I'm glad you're out here. I didn't get to say something.'

'What was that?'

'Just that I'm sorry about what happened to Vince. He was a beautiful man.'

I nodded. 'Yeah.'

'And I did love him,' she said. 'Did you know that?'

'No,' I said. 'I didn't know that.'

'Then again,' she said, 'it's not that simple, is it? I mean, I still love Tess, and things between us are terrible.'

'I know about *that*,' I said.

We were quiet again.

'What happened on that freeway?' I said at last. 'You never finished that story.'

'What freeway?'

'With Dad. Doing burnouts on the Tullamarine freeway.'

'Oh that. Yeah. We were looking for a place to shoot Mike's film,' Astra said. 'I guess I loved Mike in a way, too. He was a true believer.'

'A true believer in what?'

'Oh, you know,' she said, 'the spirit of the age, I guess. All that utopian business you still see round here for instance. How we're all gonna live in peace and sustainability ever after. We all believed it. I mean, we were really *fabulous* there for a while. Your dad included. But that's not what's going to happen, is it? We gave it a crack and now …'

'And now?'

'That's what I mean. I don't know.'

I waited for her to go on.

'I've lost my attachment to pretty much everything,' she said, making a gesture in the air with her cigarette. 'It's disconcerting. But on another level, I kind of like it. It's sort of not my business anymore, you know. And now there's this other thing, which is happening. Rhett's mates back there. And they are *different*. I mean, they are sorting through the available data in a *really* different way. For them, it's all about Mars and Elon Musk and the internet. It's all about this whole post-human thing. They want to build robots to fight wars and replace women.' She shrugged. 'That's the future.'

'You think?'

'Well, it's a thing, anyway. Look it up.'

'And what about your daughter?'

She sighed. Indra was older, she explained. 'She's your age, a totally different generation. Plus, Indra's just a really sensitive, wise sort of person.' She'd been through some hard stuff, but now she was really flourishing. Astra was trying to let her do her own thing, which seemed to be what she wanted, some space from her parents. But being so far away from her was sometimes almost unbearable, Astra said. 'A parent's love for a child, you probably know this yourself, it's pretty bottomless. It goes down into the guts of the world. But a child's love for a parent is different. It goes up. It's more ethereal. It's not quite present on the earth.'

A plane blinked past.

'Sometimes I see teenagers with their mothers,' Astra said, 'and I just think, you've got no idea how much that poor woman loves you.'

Astra stood up then and raised her hands to the sky. And just like that it occurred to me that this — this private valley — was the place she came to make contact with the UFOs. I imagined the discs swooping down, hovering in the gulf of air above us, humming and giving off their warm glow. I imagined Astra communicating in psychic waves. I must have laughed out loud.

'What?' Astra said.

'Nothing,' I said. 'I was just thinking about Dad.'

'He had a sense of humour.'

'Did he? I can't really remember.'

'No,' she said after a while. 'Neither can I, to be honest.'

12.

A few weeks later, I took the day off work and went to watch Mike Tadic's three surviving films, in a little booth at the Screen and Television Archive at Federation Square, in Melbourne. They were funny, awkward, luminous, boring films of odd lengths: thirty-seven minutes, forty-two minutes, one hundred and fifty-seven minutes. Too long, or not quite long enough, as if they were designed not to be watched at all, to fall instead through the gaps of our attention span. They were all shot in 1970 or 1971, over a period of weeks with not much money, which is to say, with every last cent of Mike's money and a small contribution from the Experimental Film and Television Fund. I'd done some research. Later, they were converted from 16mm onto VHS. These precious, faulty, amateur videos — this is our heritage. You can go see them anytime you want, although I wouldn't necessarily recommend it.

The first film jammed in the video player, and I think I might have destroyed it when I tried to pry it out. An assistant managed to find a second copy somewhere, but the sound on that one came and went, and for agonising periods I was forced to lip-read through a roar of static. Then the sound would suddenly clear, and those uncanny Australian accents from the seventies would return, so ordinary and lonely and naive. The voices of people who had no idea what was coming. Then just some very long, psychedelic dream sequences. Too long for most people's taste, I would say.

That first film was called *Ghosts*. It was the most experimental, the most interesting, and the longest. It opened with a group of hippies stumbling around for ages through a smouldering wasteland: grey sky, flute solo, sleepy guitar, and mounds of rubbish burning under an enormous half-built bridge. The soundtrack was composed by a band called Leprous Porpoise. 'Love should be put into action,' the singer moans, 'but man, I can't move, I'm just relaxin'.'

The story is simple enough. Three very different people — a doctor, a hippie, and a tender-hearted ex-con — all experience the same prophetic dream, in which the voice of a young girl calls to them from a river. Compelled to find the source of the voice, they meet each other beneath an enormous bridge one day. And here the film changes gear: the crew enters the action, and the actors step out of character. Sitting around a campfire, everyone drops acid and discusses how to finish the film. Conversations veer off; they talk about their own feelings and fears, about drugs and death and Krishnamurti, about their failed relationships, the beauty of misunderstanding, the beauty of creation, about their various attempts to let go of their own egos, the attempt to do away with the self and 'to just get closer to the centre'. And yet, one of them says, 'every time we try to adopt these sorts of concepts, like openness and liberation, it's actually meaningless, because they're only ideas in the head, and there's such a huge gap between these ideological propositions and simply being able to live them'. It goes on like this for a very long time, aimlessly, like life. I loved it, actually, for a while. A wizard rows past in a boat. Some of them kick a football. There is no resolution. While they're still talking, the camera finally moves away, past the band we can now see playing, lost in the music, in their skivvies and paisley suits, in hats and football jumpers, barefoot in the mud, stoned, beside a gigantic concrete pylon. The camera turns towards a toxic orange sun that's sinking into the bay; orange light overwhelms the film stock itself, which seems to warp in a blizzard of colour. That's the end. John Mosley praised the film's 'radical disenchantment with cinematic artifice' and saw, in its liberation from repressive narrative structures, 'a new medium for an authentic analysis of being itself'. David Stratton called it 'silly and unintelligible, and of extremely limited interest'. *Ghosts* reached the final of the 1972 Benson & Hedges Awards at the Sydney Film Festival, and then disappeared.

It was only later that I realised that the bridge, where most of the action was filmed, was the Westgate Bridge, part of which had collapsed during its construction, the year before the film was made, killing thirty-five people, including Mike's father, who was working below. The subsequent gas explosion ignited the river and sent mangled metal and mud flying in every direction. Men were killed in their tents while they ate their lunch. Men were burnt to death. Today, the bottom of this bridge is fenced off or leased by industrial manufacturing companies, and it would be difficult even to walk around there without being arrested, let alone to make a film in which everyone, including the crew, was on LSD.

The other two films were little parables disguised as something more ordinary and gritty. In the first of these I watched, *Visitations*, a bank robber called Damo is released from prison and drives around

Melbourne, visiting his old mates and trying to determine who dobbed him in to the cops. The film ends when the car crashes and everyone — Damo, together with all the possible traitors he's collected along the way — dies. The last film, *Autumn, Winter*, is about an unhappy couple who find themselves alone in a country house that's sinking into the mud. They eat, kiss, dance, sleep, argue, and mope around saying disconnected, arty things to each other. The camera dwells for long periods on the shifting leaves in the dark garden outside, the raindrops waiting to fall, while a Bach fugue plays so loudly it scorches the ears.

I watched all three films with a feeling of gathering anxiety, hoping to catch sight of a face I might recognise from my childhood — Abbie, for instance, or, better still, the face of my father as an extra in the background. But I didn't. I saw no one I knew, and I grew so weary eventually, so drained sitting there in the dark, that I forgot what it was I was supposed to be doing. I felt scraped out, drifting mindlessly, but without peace. It was all I could do just to get to the final scene of *Autumn, Winter* where the house, with the sad couple still inside, finally disappears entirely, a bit clumsily, into the mud. Two bubbles float on the surface for a few seconds, then burst. Relieved, disappointed, dehydrated, I stumbled out onto Flinders Street, into the cold air. Life! Traffic! The twenty-first century!

It turned out I actually *was* sick, and I slept terribly that night, lurching through a swamp of garish dream-films: static sequences, bad acting, scenes that repeated themselves again and again, with slight variations. It was as if there were something poisonous about all those images, something almost radioactive that needed to be purged and sweated out. Those too-bright oranges and pinks and greens. The fluttering lines of static. All those dirty, sunburnt hippies. Or perhaps it was simply that I had gone down too far into the seventies, had seen too much or come up too quickly. Maybe films measure time — or dissolve it — in ways we don't understand.

And maybe that was the reason I dreaded meeting Mike. Dreaded even calling him. In Astra's handwriting, in blue ink on a yellow sticky-note, his phone number frightened me. I had forgotten the way a telephone number can possess an aura when it's written out on a piece of paper. Sarah had given me *her* number like that, years earlier — a note handed to me surreptitiously in a crowded room — and suddenly life had swerved in a new direction. I was thinking about that moment, an otherwise dull book launch at the university, that first, startling conversation, and the way Sarah had smiled and pressed something into my hand as she turned to leave. But I was also thinking about the story Astra had mentioned: the screwdriver and the tree. And so I put off calling Mike until my own procrastination became unbearable and began to outweigh my fear. *Love should be put into action*, I thought. And in any case, the number Astra had given me was only seven digits long; she doubted it was still connected. Finally, I picked up the phone and dialled, adding a nine to the front. I was praying that Mike wouldn't answer — I almost hung up — but then he did.

Reluctantly, as if he had no choice in the matter, he told me to come and see him. He had a soft voice and a distracted, cautious manner. He gave me his address. He lived in Footscray. 'Come in the evening,' he said. 'I'm better in the evenings.'

I caught the train out later that week. I knew almost nothing about the western suburbs of Melbourne, although this was where my father had spent a few unhappy years as a teenager, crashing cars and blowing things up, and I felt a jolt of excitement to be there, as the train rose from underground into the blue twilight. Out the window I saw the moon above an expanse of dark railyards, which I didn't recognise: machinery, bridges, heavy shadows encrusted with lights like red and golden jewels, and it seemed as if the city I knew was gone and had been replaced by something else, a different city, or the same city from a distant future.

Mike opened the door wearing a tattered woollen jumper. He was a big man; big-headed, big-boned, big-eared like all old men, with close-cropped grey hair, and hands that might once have been powerful but were now more or less crippled by arthritis. He nodded and said something I didn't hear properly, *the road to Azbazan*, was what I thought he said, although he probably didn't say that, and there was a moment of awkwardness while he waited for me to respond. A white cat circled his leg and disappeared into the darkness behind him. Finally, he turned, and I followed him down the hallway into a small kitchen that smelt strongly of cigarette smoke and soup, but which wasn't particularly warm. A dim bulb on the rangehood illuminated a spattered stovetop and a sink where a pile of dishes sat half-immersed in brown liquid.

Mike mumbled something and pointed to a chair. I sat down. The table was covered in newspapers, which he began condensing nervously into three bundles of apparent significance. Later, when he was out of the room, I looked at them more closely and saw that they were all from the 1990s. The rest of the house was very dark, and it was hard to get a sense of how big it was or what it might have been like during the day. The rooms were small, I could tell that much, cluttered with the blurry shapes of books and ornaments and furniture that had presumably belonged to Mike's mother, Vesna, with who — as I would learn — he'd been living for some years. Many of the objects had an antique feel; heavy pieces of wooden furniture and, along the walls, bookshelves, black-and-white photographs, and shadows that loomed like dolls and teapots. Vesna had died the year before last, Mike told me at some point that evening, at the age of ninety-eight, and eventually I was allowed to turn the plastic pages of an old album, in which I saw photos of her smoking defiantly, her knitted cardigan littered with Communist badges, trade-union badges, environmental badges, anti-uranium badges. *Better Active Today than Radioactive Tomorrow!* She had been a powerful woman in her youth, and a fierce Communist apparently, who seemed, in these photos anyway, to grow larger as she aged until, in her nineties, still a smoker, still covered in badges, she was a sort of titan with huge arms and swollen purple ankles. She had died on a tram of a heart attack and been carried across the city, from Airport West to Elizabeth Street and back, no one knew how many times, before someone finally noticed that she was dead. Mike, who had been a tram conductor until the system was privatised in the nineties, when his job was replaced by machines, was understandably disturbed by this. I watched his face twitch as he spoke about it, but his delicate voice barely changed its modulation. And that must have been the moment that I began noticing the crucifixes. They had been attached to the walls all around us, and seemed to emerge, one by one, from the dimness, like those glow-in-the-dark stars that kids stick onto the ceiling. But whether they'd been stuck there by Mike or by his mother, I didn't ask.

—

'What was it?' Mike said, looking down at his hands. 'A green Beetle?'

We were drinking black tea, and rakia from a tall, unmarked bottle, and talking about the footage that Astra had mentioned, the footage of my dad spinning around on the Tullamarine freeway.

'Dad's car?' I said. 'No. A Monaro. A yellow Monaro.'

'Yellow? Was it?' Mike murmured. 'Bird-shit yellow? Yeah, could have been, I guess.'

This footage, those burnouts — that was what I really wanted to see. But it was long gone. At some point in the mid-seventies, Mike had destroyed everything.

Had it happened the way Astra described?

Mike stood up, took a few steps, then sat down again.

'Some of that sounds sort of right,' he said, pouring us both more rakia. 'But I don't remember Astra being there.'

'Really?'

He lit another cigarette. 'As far as I'm concerned,' he said, 'it was just me and your dad.'

'Okay,' I said, watching his face as he smoked. It was smooth, open — strangely childlike, in fact, in its openness — and yet it nevertheless suggested years of invisible damage. He was someone around who, it seemed, undecided forces continued to coalesce. Luck and its opposite circled him hungrily.

Now that I knew the footage was gone, I wasn't sure what else I could do there.

I asked Mike about the film he'd been trying to make. 'What happened to that in the end? Did you finish it?'

He looked at me for a second with what I took to be undisguised loathing. *Who is this prick*, he must have thought, *come to wake up old demons*. But he didn't say that. He just looked away, and I watched him watching his own hands in silence, stretching his big fingers back and forth to the point where the pain began or where it became too much.

But he did tell me, eventually.

The movie itself, he explained — *Strange Lands Under the Fires of Heaven* — was never made, though he did remember the plot, such as it was. A group of anarchists, pursued by a corrupt cop tentatively named 'Fucknuckle', take shelter in the mountains. One night, during a storm, they discover 'the helmsman', a grisly old hermit covered in scabs and ash, who keeps guard at a mysterious hole in the ground.

Things descend into madness. Literally. That was going to be the line on the poster, Mike explained. 'There was a guy who lived with us there in Chaucer Street, who did these great posters.'

The anarchists overpower the helmsman and then, one by one, they lower themselves into the hole.

'And then what?' I asked.

'Fucked if I know,' Mike said. 'Madness, I guess. It was a pretty strange time. But I bet everyone says that.'

At some point, the share house where he was living fell apart. He ran out of money. His camera broke. His actors disappeared or were imprisoned or died of drug overdoses. Mike entered a period that he didn't remember very well. He stopped even trying to make films. He set fire to a lot of things. The Royal Park Psychiatric Hospital, as it was known then, was a horrible place, he said. Bedlam, they used to call it. And then there was a period following that, a much happier time that he didn't remember very well either, which he spent as a voluntary outpatient at the Parkville Psychiatric Clinic under the supervision of a doctor called Dick Ball.

'Funny name,' Mike agreed, refilling my glass, 'but a lovely bloke.' Mike had walked into the doctor's office one spring day, and there on the wall was a poster of Krishnamurti. 'It was a sign.'

By this point I was struggling to focus on anything Mike was saying. We had drunk quite a lot of rakia. The room had begun to spin. And maybe *that* was when I noticed the crucifixes for the first time, gathering around me. It's hard to say now. And then I was climbing into the passenger seat of Mike's tiny Hyundai Excel. But where were we going? The quiet shops were suddenly flashing past. The gearbox roared to catch up. I remember passing Priceline, Helloworld, Home of Beauty, Chinamax, Lazy Moe's. The green lights were invisible; the red lights seemed to burn in the darkness. And then we were on the Tullamarine freeway, which was a hell of a lot bigger than it used to be, Mike told me, which was a chaos of half-finished new lanes, fresh-flowered embankments, piles of rubble and dirt, and machines slowly turning in the yellow light. The car shuddered on the unfinished tarmac as we approached the airport. Is that where he was taking me? To the airport? We passed the long-term carpark, still glowing there like an abandoned city. We passed the airport altogether. Temporary walls closed in on either side, a kind of tunnel, which suddenly fell away, and then we entered the almost absolute darkness of the paddocks.

Something had happened to Mike, I realised. It was as if a switch had been flicked in his brain. He was smiling now, or grimacing happily, he was buoyant, waving his hands in the air. He was saying something about a science fiction movie he wanted to make. And it occurred to me then that I had entrusted my life to a man who was not only very drunk, but also probably insane.

Mike pulled into a gravel carpark and switched the engine off.

I looked around.

There was a food-truck glowing in the darkness, and some kids running around in Spiderman outfits. In front of us, an immense black paddock lay glittering with garbage in the headlights of parked cars.

I tried to say something, but Mike told me to be quiet.

And then we saw it. At first I thought it was the moon emerging from behind a cloud. Slowly it flooded the air around it with light, and then it began to blink; it changed from being a moon into an object that was coming towards us. Its lights multiplied. We could hear it. It became an aeroplane driving straight at us. We got out and stood in front of the car. Mike handed me the bottle of rakia. Someone screamed. And then it was on us like surf, roaring through the darkness above our heads, its huge, naked underbelly intimate and deadly as a shark. When it passed, we turned and watched it waver like a giant horizontal crucifix, and then descend towards the pulsing lights of the runway. I remember Mike's face. He looked younger. He looked ecstatic. These aeroplanes would be in the movie too, he assured me. In fact, this is where his new film would begin, he said, holding up his fingers to simulate a tiny camera frame. 'Right here, staring at the darkness, like this.'

We sat and drank on the bonnet of the car for quite a while that night, while Mike told me about the movie he was writing. It would be called *Tullamarine*, he said, in honour of the suburb, the freeway, and the airport, which were all named after a Wurundjeri man called Tullamareena, who had resisted the British occupation and been imprisoned in the very first Melbourne gaol in 1838. Tullamareena had set fire to the roof. Then he'd lifted himself through the flaming hole and escaped, while the gaol burnt to the ground.

'What a fucking hero!' Mike exclaimed.

Now he wanted to make a film about this man, his first film in nearly fifty years, which would move in time between the 1830s and the 1990s and would astound the whole country, if only he could get the money, Mike said, if only it wasn't always the same nine or ten people who got all the money to make all the same insipid little films, year after year. Melbourne Airport had been named, however inadvertently, after an Aboriginal resistance fighter, and while it was a paltry recompense, obviously, it seemed nevertheless — and this was the logic of his film (a film I knew he would never make) — that Melbourne Airport itself was a burning prison, or the ghost of a burning prison, or some sort of secret star gate, and that by escaping in the way he did, Tullamareena had somehow punched a hole in the air and invented human flight.

'A person who has never been outside the realm of reality wouldn't understand,' Mike was saying. And though I couldn't understand *exactly* what he was talking about, I felt, I think, that I *did* understand, and that I agreed. I could sense some deep magic working through whatever we were doing there that night, protecting us. We were very drunk. We were speeding back along the Tullamarine freeway by this point, with the windows open. And if this had been a story, or a film for that matter, then we would have crashed and died for sure, because such hubris cannot be rewarded.

But we didn't. We escaped with our lives. We *were* rewarded.

13.

A few weeks after these events, I flew up to the Gold Coast for my mother's birthday. We sat at the dinner table on the seventeenth floor with Bill, and Tara, and Tara's nice husband, Gus, and their two little girls, and we got drunk and ate roast turkey because we thought we may as well pretend it was Christmas while we were at it. It was thirty-two degrees. Sarah and Sylvie stayed home.

After lunch, and after we had drunk as much of Bill's famous wine collection as we could, I found myself sitting on the floor of my mother's bedroom, hiccuping, with a few decades' worth of old photos scattered across the white carpet. And among them, of course, was the photograph of my father, looking very, very, very happy in his orange robes. My father, who I loved, suddenly, and who looked so young and beautiful. He was wearing a long set of beads around his neck, and even though his clothes were grubby, there was something radiant about him, his face, his eyes. It seemed as if he'd been washed clean. My mother had told me she had no idea where that photo had got to. But here it was. It had been in her bedroom all along. She'd also told me she didn't know anything about my father's time in the ashram. But that wasn't strictly true, either.

I found my mother in the kitchen, smiling drunkenly. She looked like an old woman, I saw now. Older and weaker, and dodderingly pleased to have both her children in the same building at once, if not all her grandchildren. Pleased, too, it seemed to me, that we'd all be gone by tomorrow evening, and that her life without us would soon begin again. She had skin like thin, crumpled paper that had been flattened out, hair that she had stopped dyeing blonde, and very tired black eyes. Tired, but also strangely canny, I thought, strangely wild. She was a survivor, my mother. She fiddled with her hearing aid and peered at me.

'You look a bit worse for wear,' she said.

'Thanks, Mum.'

I showed her the photo.

She rolled her eyes. 'You really want to do this again?' she said.

But we'd never done it. That was the whole point. We skated across the surface. It was in our blood. We reeled away whenever the charge of reality became too strong.

'Your father lived in an ashram for a month or two in 1976,' my mother said. 'He wore orange. He meditated. He sang the bloody songs. What else can I tell you?'

'What ashram?'

'The Osho ashram. That Indian bloke with all the Rolls-Royces. Bhagwan. Bag-wash, we used to call him.'

'How many Rolls-Royces did he have?'

'Oh, I can't remember,' she said. 'A hundred and something?'

So my dad had fallen in with a guru who really liked cars. Maybe that wasn't so weird.

'And then what happened?'

'Nothing,' my mother said. 'When he'd had enough, he came back to Australia. He had a friend called Havoc who was looking after Byron Street while he was away, and I knew Havoc a bit, and he put on a big surprise party to welcome Vincent home. I've told you all this. I went along because it was a party, even though I didn't know who the hell Vincent was.'

'What happened to Havoc?' I asked.

'He died ages ago,' she said. 'Some sort of brain haemorrhage. Anyway, there were all these people who knew Vincent, and they were all going: "Geez I can't wait for Vince to get home", and I was saying "Ahh fucking hell, really?" But then he turned up and we got together just like that.'

She handed me a biscuit with cheese. 'So there you go,' she said. 'Happy?'

'Was Dad still wearing orange when you guys got together?'

'No,' she said. 'He'd renounced by that stage.'

'Renounced? Are you serious? Why do I not know this?'

'You do. You know all this. I keep telling you the same thing over and over again.'

'You never said the word "renounced".'

'You're like me,' she said. 'You're very vague. You don't listen properly.'

'But what happened? Did something happen that made him renounce?'

'Why do you think something must have happened?' my mother said. 'He just grew out of it, like the rest of them. It'd be a bit boring being in a cult, don't you reckon?'

She began stacking the dishwasher.

'Rinse those, would you,' she said, pointing to a pile of dirty plates on the bench.

I did, and then I leant against the fridge and Googled *osho bhagwan ashram* on my phone. There were people weeping in long lines. There were lots of semi-naked people with their hands in the air. There were men in pink jumpsuits with semi-automatic weapons. They were all wearing the same necklace my father had worn in the photo, a set of wooden beads with a little image of the guru at one end. I read the words 'Sex-Cult'. I saw Osho's smiling face and those eyes of his. He looked pretty happy. But were they the eyes of a master or a villain? I couldn't tell.

'So it says here they poisoned people, Mum.'

'Oh yeah,' she laughed, 'but that was after your dad's time.'

Later, while everyone else was watching *The Little Mermaid*, I stood beside Tara at those big windows, looking down as the tiny surfers battled their tiny waves. From this height, all human suffering appeared comically insignificant, and maybe that was part of the attraction. Tara threw her arm around my shoulder, mock seriously, and drew me to her.

'So hi,' she said.

We hadn't seen each other for a year. I'd missed her.

'Did you know Dad was in a cult?' I said.

'You mean that Osho thing?'

I pulled away. 'How do *you* know about that?'

Tara shrugged. 'Is it supposed to be a secret?'

'Yes. No one ever told me.'

'Ah well, I guess,' she said. 'Anyway, how's Sylvie?'

'Sylvie's fine,' I said, bringing up an image of Osho on my phone. 'Sylvie's great. You know how it is.' I handed her the phone. 'What does this picture make you think of?'

She glanced at it. 'It makes me think of Dad, I guess. And, like, I don't know, mass-suicide or something?'

'And?'

But that was all. Tara didn't actually know any more than I did. She didn't know how long Dad had been there, or what he thought about the whole thing, or why he'd left and never mentioned it again. It didn't seem to interest her very much.

'I just sort of assumed everyone was into that stuff in the seventies,' she said.

And then we began talking about something else.

'You look tired,' she said.

'Thank you.'

'Seriously, Joe. Are you okay? Because, really, you look a bit like shit.'

14.

On YouTube, a few days later, I found this:

Hundreds of semi-naked westerners; bearded, beautiful, hairy, orange-clad people hard at work in a jungle of dappled light. It was the ashram in Pune in 1976. The year my father was there.

Sylvie was asleep. Sarah was in bed, probably not asleep. I was sitting on the couch, in darkness. It was nearly midnight. There were plenty of Osho's lectures I could have watched. I had, in fact, watched some of them. You can watch them yourself. Bhagwan on 'Life' and 'Laughter' and then — after he changed his name — Osho on everything else: on 'Love' and 'Happiness' and 'Death' and 'Marriage'. Osho sitting in a chair that appeared to be made entirely from bubble-wrap. Osho looking increasingly bitter, it seemed to me, looking less and less trustworthy. I recognised his face from some distant region of my childhood, his unblinking eyes, his slow, soft, hissing way of speaking. I could not help liking him. I even felt myself wanting to *love* him, weird as that sounds. And yet I couldn't look at him properly, either. I didn't want to. I wasn't ready for any of it. And so it was just this little film, a few minutes of silent Super-8 footage, that did something to me that night, that slipped past me and took me by surprise. The images pulsed like something that was alive. People moved through hanging pools of light. Images of women dancing or screen-printing or pouring enormous silver bowls of milk. Images of men, who all looked, it's true, like Charles Manson, gardening or riding bicycles or repairing drainpipes. And yet, they didn't *look* like brainwashed psychopaths. It didn't look like alienated labour, like drudgery. The whole place looked like a vast artist's studio, and the aura of sex clung to everyone. *If nothing else*, I thought, *utopia is a quality of dappled light like this*. I was looking for my father somewhere amid the crowds, the image of my father come back to life. I didn't see him, but at three minutes and forty-six seconds I saw a glimmer of long blonde hair, a beautiful man in red overalls doing ... what? Cutting wood? Measuring something? I couldn't tell. It lasted barely a second. It was like an image from a dream. It was Abbie.

15.

So my father was no longer an orange person — a *sannyasin* — when my parents met, although apparently they both knew plenty of people who were. Like Abbie, for instance. Like Abbie's old girlfriend Rani. *They* were still wearing orange well into the 1980s.

'You remember Rani, don't you?' my mother had said. 'She used to babysit you.'

Now Rani lived in San Francisco with her second husband. She and my mum had stayed in touch. Rani's first husband, Dave, had died a few years earlier, and they had a son together, called Asha, who I faintly remembered. Rani had left Asha with Dave and gone back to live with Bhagwan, in Oregon. So the story went. At some point Bhagwan had moved to America, to a big ranch in the middle of nowhere. The last time I saw Asha, he was an inconsolable child of four or five. Now he was thirty-eight years old and six-foot-seven, my mother said, a silent giant who lived alone in a shack that he'd built for himself near Torquay. He surfed, and hunted, and butchered his own deer.

Deer? I thought. Jesus Christ, who even knew there were deer in Australia?

I found Rani's website and emailed her. She was a photographer. Three days later, on a packed train, coming home from work, I got a reply:

It was so lovely to get your email, Rani wrote. *Of course I remember babysitting you. Of course I remember the ashram. But maybe we can speak about this over the phone.*

Rani had lived in the ashram in India for four years, she told me, and she still considered it the happiest time of her life. *And yes,* she wrote, *your dad was there, too. That's where I met him. His name at the time was Swami Anand Komalatva. Swami means 'master'. Anand means 'bliss'. Komalatva means 'tenderness'.*

16.

I called Rani a few days later. It was past midnight in Melbourne, and seven-thirty in the morning where Rani was in San Francisco — which was pretty much what we'd arranged. I'd gone out and got drunker than I'd planned, but now I was home again. I was standing in the kitchen. Rani answered on the third ring. Her accent disconcerted me; part Australian, part English, part American, and part something else I couldn't place, but she laughed easily, and I liked her immediately for that.

'I met your dad at the ashram,' she told me. 'I watched him get reborn.'

'Okay,' I said. 'I mean, what?'

'I thought you'd like that,' she laughed.

My father had lain on the floor, hyperventilating, while Rani sat behind him, guiding him with implacable calmness through the traumatic memory of his own birth. They were both naked.

'Not that there was anything going on between us,' she clarified. 'I was involved with Abbie in those days, and Abbie and your dad were great friends.'

'Okay,' I said. 'Sure. But what was it like? What was Bhagwan like?'

'Pune, the actual city,' she said, 'was a horrible little place in those days. But all the other stuff is true.' By which she meant all the good stuff: the pure love that emanated from Bhagwan, the trees, the air, the light, human relations, everything. She fell in love with Bhagwan, she said, like everyone else. She remembered wondering if she'd actually been depressed all her life. She had gladly traded her previous name, Mary, for Rani, which meant 'queen'. Bhagwan had touched her forehead, and she had begun to shake and weep. 'I think something similar must have happened to your dad,' Rani said. 'The difference being that he hated that name, Komalatva.'

'And what was Abbie's name?' I asked.

'Abbie's name was Abhi,' she said. 'A.B.H.I. Swami Prem Abhiyāna.'

She waited while I found a pen, and then she spelt it out for me.

'There's a little thing over the top of that second *a*,' she said. 'A little line. I can't remember what that's called. But Swami means "master of yourself" and Prem means "love" and Abhiyāna means "divine adventure". Abhi for short. His name before that was Kurt.'

Kurt.

Had I known that?

Suddenly I was sitting on a bed with my back against the wall; a fleeting memory from a part of childhood I had otherwise forgotten. I was in a small wooden house beside a highway. It was Abhi's house, this much I knew, though it seemed less a memory, really, than a state of light. My parents had driven for a long time to get there, although I didn't remember the drive, only a vague sense of being exhausted after it, and of being frightened, alarmed by the strangeness of the night, the blackness of the surrounding countryside, by the fact that I was awake at an hour when I was usually asleep, in a forbidden territory. The light in the room was orange — there must have been a fire — and above the fireplace was a round fish-eye mirror. But maybe I was making that up. Even the presence of my parents was only an assumption, or a faint image-feeling. Maybe the only thing that could have truly been called a memory was the light — overwhelmingly orange — and the fact that Abhi was there, somewhere, just out of reach.

'What else did you used to do?' I asked.

'What do you mean?' Rani said.

'In the ashram. It was a cult, wasn't it?'

'Of course it was a cult,' she said, laughing again. 'It was fucking great. We did everything. That was the point. It was wild. "Just be total", Bhagwan used to say.'

'Then why did Dad leave? Did something happen?'

There was a pause on the end of the phone.

'Yeah,' Rani said at last. 'Yeah, you know, I think something *did* happen. But I don't know what it was. Suddenly he and Abhi were both gone.'

Two months later, she told me, Abhi returned to the ashram, by himself.

So I was right. Something *had* happened that made Dad leave.

'But you'd have to ask Abhi about that,' Rani said.

'I have,' I said. 'I've tried. He doesn't want to talk to me.'

'I'll have a word to him,' Rani said. 'You know, I can remember your dad wrote us a letter from Australia to say you'd been born and would we be your godparents. He'd changed his name back to Vincent by that stage. I'm your godmother, I think. Did you know that?'

'No,' I said. 'I didn't.'

'I guess I've been a bit absent,' Rani said.

There was another pause. I didn't ask Rani how it felt to have abandoned her *actual* child all those years ago. In a way, I felt I already knew the answer. Or, I already *almost* knew the answer. I already knew that it was possible to do such a thing, and that a part of you must close like a fist to do it. Earlier that evening, before I'd left the house, I had sat for a minute, watching Sylvie while she played on the carpet with a bowl of wooden fruit. She had annoyed me for most of the day, or, at the very least, I had found myself for most of the day simply enduring her. But in that moment, she glowed and shielded me from Sarah, who had just come home from work, and who I had avoided looking at for the past forty-eight hours.

'I have to go,' I'd told Sarah, standing up abruptly and walking past her, towards the front door. Then I came back and stooped to kiss Sylvie on her small, dark head. Her heady-head-head.

'These are the apples,' Sylvie said to no one in particular, 'but I call them children. And this is the mumma. And the dadda has gone to have some beer.'

17.

The months passed. Sylvie turned four. I spent every Friday with her, pushing swings in the park and staring at my phone like an idiot. I couldn't help it. We jumped from rock to rock. We didn't step on the cracks. We built little nests in the roots of trees, and collected seeds and bits of fluff, and broken pieces of shiny plastic that I found weeks later in the pockets of all my jackets. If it rained, we went to the museum, but it hardly ever rained. Once, we went to a climate-change rally, where Sylvie held a sign, and got bored and hot, and wanted to leave before the speeches had even begun.

'Pretend we're mechanics now,' she said.

'We're mechanics now,' I said.

We edged our way back through the crowd. But we weren't mechanics. We were deserters. We went and got ice-cream instead.

As she was falling asleep that night, Sylvie turned to me.

'Dad,' she said.

'Yes, mate?'

'I want to go back and do it all again, this day.'

—

On all the other days of the week, my work at the university continued. I wrote my press releases. I organised interviews, and arranged for journalists to write articles about the university's groundbreaking research. I had always wanted to be a journalist, and for a few years, I had been, so I knew exactly what they should say. I spoonfed them, and yet, it often seemed to me that my job consisted, for the most part, of making something that hadn't happened yet, and which probably never would, seem like an achievement of truly global significance. The respect the university pretended to have for its students and its academic staff, meanwhile, was matched almost perfectly by the disdain in which it actually held them. It wanted their money, and the prestige when they succeeded, but not the inconveniences associated with real human endeavour, or with the work of actually teaching, for that matter. Morale was low. The senior lecturers who came to my office complained endlessly. A monstrous corporate culture was trying to destroy everything they loved and believed in. It sounded like a conspiracy theory, except it was true. I agreed with everything they said, and yet there were times, in the middle of these conversations, or in departmental meetings, when I would suddenly hear the word *Komalatva*, like a whisper at the back of my mind, like a kind of dizziness. *Komalatva*. *Tenderness*. My father's ridiculous name. And then I would excuse myself, as if directed by an unknown force, and walk down the corridor and out onto the artificial grass and call the only person who could tell me what I needed to know. Abhi.

But he never answered the phone.

'He's gone back to India,' Rani told me when I emailed her again.

'God knows why.' She had spoken to him not long before he left.

I asked her how I could reach him, and she sent me a dubious Yahoo address. He was living in Kerala now, she told me. She didn't know what he was doing. I wrote him a bunch of emails when I should have been writing other emails. I lied and said I might be coming through Bengaluru (formerly Bangalore) for a work conference, and could I come and say hi? He didn't respond.

Did Rani have his address by any chance? I told her I wanted to send him a postcard.

A few days later, she sent me the name of a café a few hundred metres from Varkala Beach. The Café le Space.

'That's all he gave me,' Rani said.

On the internet I saw photos of a plain, open-air restaurant connected to an ageing resort. I saw photos of people's food, and tourists hugging one another, red-eyed in the camera flash, and a dirty beach where men were pouring piles of small silver fish onto the sand. I stared at the blurry roofs of beach resorts on Google Earth, and the frozen waves that had been caught, mid-dash, by satellite camera. And then one day, when I should have been doing something else, I booked a flight to India. I set about making plans to be in Kerala in a month's time.

18.

'India,' Sarah said when I told her. 'What a fucking cliché. Do you even realise you're having a midlife crisis?'

Still, she agreed to drive me to the airport, so that Sylvie could say goodbye and see the aeroplanes. I didn't know how long I'd be gone. In my mind I gave myself a couple of weeks. A month at most. I'd taken a month off work. More than long enough, I assumed, to find Abhi and make him tell me whatever he knew about the ashram. Whatever he knew about my father, and my father's guru. There was no one left to ask.

And so, three weeks later, we stood in the terminal together, Sarah, Sylvie, and I. My little family. The crowds parted around us.

'I'll be back soon,' I said.

'Very soon,' Sylvie said.

'Yeah,' Sarah said, 'good for you.'

We stared at each other without saying anything for a moment, two damaged planets teeming with incompatible life. Even in my bitterness, she had never stopped being beautiful to me. Then she turned away, and we watched in silence as Sylvie skipped towards the tinted windows. For a second I thought about calling the whole thing off, but I didn't, and soon I had turned away as well and was walking towards those big silver gates, which open to let you leave but through which you can never return. I was thinking about Tullamareena, who had set fire to the first Melbourne gaol, who had climbed up through a burning hole in the roof and escaped to freedom.

Gradually, the shimmering calm at Gate 3 dissolved into babble, and soon enough we had boarded. Soon we were flying through the air. I drank tiny vodkas, one after the other, and let myself be drawn into an old euphoria. I pressed my face to the greasy window where someone before me had pressed theirs. Outside the window, clouds were occurring. Above the surface of the planet, a day was passing without humans, slow and dignified. Then I switched on my screen and watched *Blade Runner 2049*, twice. I slept, and when I woke it was still going.

'Daddy, Daddy, Daddy,' a little girl called from somewhere behind me.

'It's illegal to use real memories, officer,' a woman on the screen said.

My head hurt. I wanted to go back to the little house at the start of the film, with its old piano, its humble gas stove and the smell of boiling garlic, but Ryan Gosling had set it all on fire.

PART TWO

Vincent wakes confused in The Celestial Lake, a very dirty hotel, which at least has the benefit of a ceiling fan, though it isn't moving now. The power must be out. He lies staring at the grimy blades for a while, letting the shock of his predicament run through him.

From the street outside, he hears an almost unbelievable noise: horns, motorbikes, cows, bike-bells, donkeys, rickshaws, men yelling and spitting. Sounds that had somehow tangled in his sleep with the sounds of his childhood — his father and his brother, more specifically — many years earlier, arguing in the kitchen outside his teenage bedroom. A kind of nightmare, if he's honest.

In the other bed, on the far side of the room, a man is snoring lightly, his impressive chest rising and falling. The American. Kurt.

Vincent lets the dream dissolve, like weak poison, into the day, which is swelling around him now. He looks at his watch. It's almost nine in the morning.

The room is pale green, the walls spotted with dead mosquitoes and gashes of dry red liquid. He gets up and goes to the window to look out at this new city.

Poona.

Fuck.

The street below thrums with an intensity that frightens him. Less so than Bombay, but still. Just as dusty and hectic and poor by the looks of it. Just as desperate. He feels, acutely, again, his own insignificance, the thinness of his own being. How easily he might not exist at all. He thinks: *What the fuck am I doing here?*

Vincent had arrived in darkness the night before, with two Canadians and Kurt, an American actor who had played a centurion in the stage production of *Jesus Christ Superstar*. He had met them all by chance two days earlier, at the Leopold Café, in Bombay. But the taxi bearing them down to Poona had conked out, and they'd had to wait five hours beside the road for the driver's friend (or was it his cousin?) to appear with another car. The driver had been so upset that they couldn't bring themselves to abandon him. By the time they'd found the ashram, it was after ten and the gates were closed for the night. The hotel — The Celestial Lake — was Kurt's idea. He was paying for it. The whole thing was Kurt's idea, in fact. Being here now.

Kurt talked a lot — in this he was a typical Yank — and he might have been annoying, but somehow he wasn't. He had something about him that Vincent liked immediately, against his better judgement. Americans, by definition, were agents of imperialist capitalism but Kurt, who had been among the thousands watching Abbie Hoffman trying to make the Pentagon levitate, was far more politically astute than Vincent had assumed, and more radical.

'You shoulda seen it,' Kurt had told them. 'I nearly got trampled to death by Buddhist monks.'

'And did it actually levitate?' Mitch asked credulously.

'I swear to God,' Kurt laughed, holding up his fingers to indicate maybe a quarter of an inch.

Vincent had tried to remember what year that had been. 1967? '68? '69? Abbie Hoffman was an inspiration to them all. They raved about other things. Ram Dass. Tim Leary. The psychedelic experience.

This was all at the Leopold Café, that first afternoon.

Vincent had been sketching rough portraits of the people around him, seated at a table by himself, trying not to look lonely but listening in, secretly, to the conversation that was taking place beside him. Kurt was recounting a complicated story about the Hindu gods and their vehicles. Finally, Vincent had summoned the courage to ask if he could join them.

'Absolutely,' Kurt had said, moving his satchel from the unoccupied chair. 'You're from Australia, right, let me guess …' He closed his eyes. 'Melbourne?'

Vincent was taken aback. 'How can you tell?'

'Shit man, you can tell a mile off,' Kurt said, beaming.

'Really?' No one he'd met in India knew anything about Australia, let alone Melbourne.

Kurt laughed, pointing. 'It says it on your T-shirt. "Melbourne Paranoid Degenerates Against the War". Nice one.'

Vincent laughed too. He had forgotten he was wearing that T-shirt, which Astra had made for his birthday two years earlier. Red and black. He shook hands with the Canadians — Mark and Mitch — and took a seat.

'So,' Kurt said, turning to him with a look of genuine interest. 'Tell us the story. What brings *you* to Bombay?'

It was as easy as that. Suddenly, the world was opening up again. Mitch and Mark ordered more beer. The waiters brought it. Not cold, but not definitively warm either. They exchanged anecdotes, travel wounds, epiphanies. But it was Kurt they looked to and directed their observations towards, and who held them together. He began speaking about the apathy back in the States, the way people seemed only half-alive. Mitch and Mark nodded like they understood. They were big, hairy, good-natured kids, openly confused to be in India, and Vincent liked them too. In any case, he had loved sitting there with them all, talking English, cracking jokes, and understanding everything that was being said. He liked being part of a group again — the swagger of it, the ease. He hadn't wanted to admit how incredibly lonely he had been the last few weeks, tromping around by himself, looking at everything but never feeling like he was touching anything.

Vincent had been travelling for five weeks by this time. An embarrassingly short period he remained vague about whenever people asked. And they always asked. 'Not long,' he would say, as if 'not long' might mean a couple of years. 'A few months,' he would say if he was drawn. He was looking forward to the time when that, at least, wouldn't be a lie. One month and eight days was the truth.

Still, he'd seen some things in that time. Terrible things that he felt changed by. And he was starting to look the part. He'd grown his moustache like Frank Zappa, and his hair, too, was almost as long as he wanted it to be. He was tanned and dirty, and he'd turned wiry, walking everywhere, and not eating much, and shitting water during one particularly long fever in an expensive hotel with a round bed and a mirrored roof. He looked like he knew what he was doing. Truth was though, he didn't. He felt like an impostor. Sometimes, in the middle of the day, wandering aimlessly through another dusty street, he would catch himself almost wanting to cry.

Vincent was heading to Goa next; that was the plan. The Canadians were thinking about Kathmandu. Kurt was on his way down south to see some guru in an ashram. Kurt's girlfriend was already there, apparently, an Australian girl called Mary. Kurt opened a battered book — Ram Dass's *Be Here Now* — and took out a photograph of a good-looking girl with her arms in the air. The Canadians laughed approvingly. Kurt passed round a picture of the guru. Some stinky old bloke with a beard. The whole thing sounded insane, although the Canadians seemed into it.

'Tantra,' someone said, and they started talking about girls they'd slept with. Vincent laughed and drank his beer. He could have pulled out his own photo at that point. It crossed his mind, though it would have been a lie. Astra walking naked along the beach. A black-and-white photo from New Year's Eve, which he kept tucked at the back of his notebook. But Astra was gone. She was not his. The photo was almost two years old now, and it only hurt to look at it.

So this was the story. Back in Melbourne, in a moment of desperation, Vincent had rolled the dice. He'd been reading *The Dice Man* at the time, was half-living by it, and anyway, he had to go somewhere, he had to get out of Melbourne for a while. Adelaide was one. America was five. India was six. The extreme edge of everything. He'd rolled a six.

So here he was.

But the reality was so much harder than he had imagined. He didn't love travelling around like this, it turned out. He didn't love the chaos, or the heat. He didn't like being lost. He did not feel holy just being here. The hash was good, but his inevitable paranoia wasn't. He lived in almost constant anxiety that something horrible would happen; the essential incomprehensibility of the place alarmed him, not least the fact of a society that let so many people live and die in unimaginable poverty. But maybe such thoughts were themselves a misunderstanding. Maybe Australia was the aberration. Maybe *this* was the real world. But these were half-thoughts, and he didn't interrogate them too closely. They swirled in a general feeling of inadequacy and rage that trailed him everywhere. It was as if he were loitering at the edge of his own life, waiting for the real thing to begin.

So maybe this was it, he'd thought, this ashram.

The real thing.

He had meditated a bit back in Melbourne, when Havoc was running those TM groups in the front room at Byron Street. He had whispered a secret mantra, though nothing much had happened, and an ashram wasn't something he'd ever seriously considered. He wasn't sure he even knew what an ashram was.

Kurt had interrupted this reverie, slapping him on the back.

'What about you, Vince? You in?'

'Yeah, fuck it,' Vincent laughed. 'Let's do it.'

Vincent waits for Kurt to wake up. But Kurt doesn't wake up, and Vincent goes out to find the shower, which is in another room just off the common area. A metal tank with a pull-chain. A short gush of cold water. Big cockroaches that scuttle away.

Kurt is still asleep when he comes back. Vincent dresses. Makes some noise. Clears his throat.

Kurt wakes at last. He's been talking in his sleep.

'What time is it?' he asks.

'Late,' Vincent says. 'Twenty to ten.'

'Far out.' Kurt sits up, blinks, runs his hands through his hair. 'That was the weirdest dream.' Then he claps his hands together, beams his big white grin. 'You ready, amigo?'

He springs onto the floor and begins a long series of push-ups.

Vincent folds his clothes while he waits. Then he counts his money and checks his passport. The thin gold letters on the cover are faintly reassuring. He repacks his backpack. Kurt is doing pull-ups from the doorframe now, panting theatrically, still topless. Annoyed, Vincent leaves him to it, goes and smokes a thin Indian cigarette on the balcony, overlooking a sea of rooftops, grey and half-visible in the smog. Then he goes and shits and feels a bit better.

When Kurt is finally ready, washed and shining, they walk down the corridor to collect Mark and Mitch from the next room. Then they eat breakfast together, standing on the street. Some spicy fried potatoes from a wooden cart. They're sweating through their shirts already, and a crowd has gathered around to watch them. Vincent shares his food with a little girl and the baby she is carrying on her hip.

Another ciggie squatting beside the road, with a cup of sweet, milky tea.

He'd love a proper fucking coffee.

They throw their brittle ceramic cups onto the road like everyone else, where an ancient woman sweeps them up with a straw broom. There are people everywhere. It's like an endless river of people.

An old man is sleeping in the dirt to one side, his shrivelled dick exposed to the passing traffic. There's the smell of petrol and piss and dust and frying oil and smoke.

More kids come to watch them, smiling, laughing.

Kurt commandeers two rickshaws and they get in, he and Vincent in the first, then Mark and Mitch in the second.

Kurt has an address, which his girlfriend, Mary, sent him.

'17 Koregaon Park,' he tells the driver.

Seventeen is Vincent's lucky number. Seventeen was the number of the horse, Transformer, on which he won the deposit for the house in Byron Street. Everything he has, really, he owes to that number.

His luck is starting to change. He can feel it.

Their driver spits into the dirt and says something to the other driver. Then they're off, swept recklessly along with the traffic, past crowds of pedestrians, men pulling wooden carts, shopkeepers, chickens in cages, dogs, goats, cows, broken huts, street fires, rubbish, all of it rushing past in a whirl. The wind dries their sweat. The sky is pale blue. A few smoky clouds sit low on the horizon. They slip through the gaps in the traffic. Now that they are a part of it, the mess of vehicles begins to make sense.

Kurt has his girlfriend's sweat-softened letter in his hand. Kurt had shown it to Vincent, in the hotel room the night before.

I don't know what I'm doing, Mary had written. *It's impossible to explain. I can only talk about surrender.*

Mary has changed her name. Now her name is *Rani*.

'Took me ages to figure out who the fuck *Rani* was supposed to be,' Kurt had said, laughing. But there was something weird about his laughter, Vincent had noticed, and it's not clear now whether or not Rani is expecting him or what the exact terms of their relationship might be.

The rickshaw accelerates into space, grinding its gears. Kurt is visibly anxious, and it pleases Vincent to see a glint of weakness in the American's otherwise imperturbable confidence.

They rush through the morning light. A squall of horns. The driver berates another driver. For the first time since he arrived in India, Vincent is overwhelmed by happiness.

The ashram is in a secluded back street lined with large stately houses and banyan trees that drop their roots straight down through the air like living ropes. There is a misunderstanding about the fare, a brief altercation between Mark and the second driver, which Kurt smooths away by paying the extra amount himself. And then the four men are standing at the gates, in green, almost aquatic light. A sense of peace, of coolness, like a parallel universe, even before they have entered the place.

Shree Rajneesh Ashram, the gate says.

'Cool.'

Beams of dusty sunlight slanting down through the trees. A few exotic-looking Europeans in orange and pink are standing around talking in their serious accents or hugging one another. Big smiles, everyone a bit stoned-looking. Europeans with no underpants on, according to Kurt. Underpants block the energy.

Above them, dozens of green parrots screech and dart between the trees.

And then just like that, they are beyond the gates, among more people, a crazy bunch of westerners all wandering around with the same loose looks on their faces.

Flute music drifts over from somewhere. Vincent feels like laughing. He feels like a fucking Beatle. He flashes a comical peace sign at Kurt, wide-eyed, but it doesn't seem to register. Kurt is preoccupied; he's headed for a glass-fronted office to the right. Mitch and Mark have wandered away in another direction. Further in, the place seems like a maze, a rabbit warren.

From a darkened doorway, Vincent sees two women emerge. Beautiful women. They are both wearing orange headscarves and clean orange aprons above light-pink shirts. They come walking towards him, perfectly in step with each other, and one of them is carrying something ceremoniously in front of her. But what?

A decapitated head.

For half a second, the image is real.

But no. It's a watermelon.

As they pass, the woman with the watermelon catches his eye, smiles, holds his gaze, as if daring him to say something. It's a look that is bright with secret knowledge. Vincent turns to watch her, struck now with a powerful sense of déjà vu. It's as if a slide has clicked into place in a projector, and come into focus. A memory of Astra looking at him, just like that.

This is more like it, he thinks. Fucking hell. Maybe he *has* come to the right place, after all.

He finds Kurt in a blast of air-conditioning, in the office on the corner, waiting to talk to an Indian woman. The woman is sitting on a platform behind a glass desk, smiling, dark-eyed, playful. There are a number of other women, westerners mostly, all dressed in orange, talking softly to other people in European accents, but this little Indian woman is clearly the boss.

Finally, it's Kurt's turn. Vincent follows him over. They sit down beside each other.

'Do you know someone called *Ma Deva Rani*?' Kurt asks.

He has memorised the full name, but he turns the piece of paper to show the woman Mary's letter. He has carried it with him all the way from California, he tells her. Also, he has a photo, which he takes out. Mary with her arms in the air.

The woman laughs warmly. Yes, she does know Rani. But Rani is in the middle of a group and cannot be disturbed.

'Would you like to leave a message?' she asks.

'Sure,' Kurt says. 'Yeah, great,' and he writes down the name of their hotel, The Celestial Lake, and their room number.

Then the woman turns to Vincent.

'So here you are,' she says unblinkingly, as if she has known him from somewhere and has been waiting for him. 'You are from Australia, yes?'

How does she know? he wonders. He checks his T-shirt, which is plain blue and gives nothing away. 'Yeah,' he says. 'I am.'

'Very good,' the woman says, watching him closely.

They have missed discourse this morning, she informs them. Discourse begins at 8am.

'Come tomorrow,' she says. 'It costs five rupees.' Somehow it doesn't feel like they're being given a choice. They pay, and receive little tickets. Then she instructs them to each write a letter of introduction to Bhagwan, and to come back in three days' time, at a quarter to six in the evening, for *darshan*.

'Darshan? What's that?' asks Vincent.

'A meeting with *Him*.' the woman explains, suddenly serious. 'An auspicious view. I think you're ready for *sannyas*, yes? Laxmi will arrange it.'

Laxmi. It seems that she is referring to herself in the third person. 'But please wash first,' she says. 'You must not smell of smoke or perfume or anything else. This is very important. *He* is very allergic.'

He being Bhagwan. The guru. The living God.

'Oh yeah. Okay. No worries.'

Sitting in dappled shade at a wooden table later that afternoon, Vincent begins his letter to the Guru.

> Dear Bhagwan,
>
> ~~G'day~~
>
> So, I don't really know what I'm doing here. I've done some Transcendental Meditation (TM) in the past, but not much. I am 25 years old. Formerly, I worked in the Prison Department for the state government, in Victoria, in Australia, working with prisoners out on parole, but I recently quit that ~~because my boss is~~ due to some disagreements with the management. ~~I am currently unemployed.~~ I have been in India for almost six weeks. I don't really know how long I'm going to be here for. I'm thinking about going into the building trade when I return to Australia. Or maybe carpentry. I'd like to work for myself. I like to work with my hands.
>
> Also, I'm not really sure if this is relevant but I have

spent some time in a psychiatric hospital (two months) for depression relating to the end of a relationship.

What I really would like to know is: what is the meaning of life? I think about this a lot. I have so many other questions. For instance, why is there so much rage inside me? Can you give me any clues? Does God exist? ~~Why does it feel like my soul is entwined in shit?~~ Who will show me how to love and live?

I guess that's it for now.

I look forward to meeting you.

All the best,

Vincent (Vince) (From Australia)

He makes a clean copy, then delivers it to the woman, Laxmi, in the office. She has a smile that reminds him of something good, though he cannot think what it is. He likes her a lot.

Somewhat disconcerted, the Canadians have retreated to a nearby hotel, The Blue Diamond, to drink. This is where Vincent and Kurt find them that evening. Two big men, tilting sideways in their chairs, drunkenly flushed and boisterous. When they see Kurt and Vincent, they stand up loudly to embrace them.

Kurt has tracked down Rani. She is living in a little room not far from the ashram, although she is in the middle of some sort of 'encounter group' at the moment, and can't talk to him.

'Two more days to go,' Kurt says. 'She doesn't want to break her concentration.'

'Why? What would happen?'

'It's like surgery,' Kurt explains. 'You can't just get up and leave in the middle of it. They have to stitch you up again.'

'What's the group?' Vincent asks.

There are about ninety therapy groups, and it's compulsory to do some of them, apparently. According to Bhagwan, therapy is necessary, because people have forgotten how to be religious. It's like purging. Around the ashram this is known as 'working on your shit'.

'Tantra,' Kurt says.

The Canadians exchange a look. 'That's the sex group, right? Is she screwing around?' Mitch asks.

Kurt shrugs, seemingly unfazed.

'Everyone is screwing around,' Mark says. 'Haven't you noticed? Just today, I saw these two people going at in the bathroom! I was like, damn! But then they turned around and man, they were *old*!'

Afterwards, while they stand outside in the smoggy evening, Kurt asks Vincent what he thinks he should do. Kurt is having second thoughts about the whole thing. Maybe he should leave, head back up to the Himalayas, forget all about Mary, Rani, whoever the hell she is.

'What do *you* want to do?' Kurt asks. 'Will you come up to the mountains with me?'

'If you go to the Himalayas, I'll come,' Vincent says. 'Yeah. Of course. But I think we should stay and see what happens.'

Kurt and Vincent get up early the next morning, leaving the Canadians to sleep. The same ritual. Breakfast standing on the street. Crowds, heat, chaos. A feeling of deep camaraderie has opened between them that seems out of proportion to the actual time they have known each other. They climb into a rickshaw.

Vincent gives the address.

17 Koregaon Park.

This time the driver doesn't bother to rip them off.

Outside the gates at this hour they can hear the sound of screaming. They hear it even before the rickshaw jolts to a stop, and it's not hard to find the source of the sound — an open-sided pavilion to the left of the front gate, where an orange mass of semi-naked westerners is literally vibrating. A hundred people at least, many of them blindfolded. They are shrieking and crying. Some of them are writhing on the ground, kicking their legs like children having tantrums.

'Jesus fucking Christ,' Kurt says. 'This is madness.'

What this is, they learn, is stage two of dynamic meditation. Next there will be ten minutes of jumping up and down, then ten minutes of stillness, and, finally, ten minutes of celebration: dancing, slow swaying, that sort of thing.

They watch it happen.

Vincent doesn't know what to think. He both wants and doesn't want what these people seem to have: their energy, and freedom, and sexual openness. His natural instinct is to get the hell out. But out *is* hell. That's exactly where he's come from.

At last the pavilion empties, and people wander away to shower, to drink tea or eat breakfast. Music plays. Other people come in to mop the sweaty floor. Surrounded by steaming gardens, Kurt and Vincent sit in the morning sun, watching it all unfold and feeling conspicuously unconverted in their ordinary, non-orange clothes: Vincent in his patched jeans and boots, despite the heat; Kurt with his white shirt unbuttoned to his belly. No matter what happens with Rani, Kurt has made up his mind to stay for another week at least. At least until he has met Bhagwan.

They talk quietly about things back home, the chances of meaningful revolution, the problems of pollution and overcrowding, the future of space exploration. Kurt is obsessed with the moon landing. They both remember where they were when they watched it happening on TV.

'I just can't get over it,' Kurt laughs. 'They went all that way just to touch it. That's what I love the most. It's so absurd.'

It's easier without the Canadians, and Vincent finds himself talking about Astra. How she'd left him. How she'd been sleeping with her therapist. He explains the slight limp he has now — the tablets he took one night, the whiskey he drank, the circulation that was cut off when he passed out. He talks about the psych hospital where he was treated, and the calliper he had to wear on his leg for months, the pins that went through his foot, the metal brace that helped him to walk. He has never told anyone about this, at least not in such detail.

They both have older brothers they don't get along with, and fathers that they more or less despise. Vincent's dad the minister; Kurt's dad the fucking war hero. It feels to Vincent as if they have known each other for years. He is not choosing his words. He is simply talking, laughing, enjoying himself, like an American, it occurs to him. The ashram seems to have infected him with well-being.

Afterwards, they join a long line snaking back into the same open-air pavilion — Buddha Hall — for 'discourse'. To get in, they have to walk in single file between two women, westerners, who lean in as they pass to sniff them. They have washed with odourless soap.

Vincent has not had a cigarette all morning, and he is irritated now at having to wait in line, with the possibility of being rejected. But they pass through with no trouble. There are perhaps two hundred people here, quite a few Indians but mostly westerners, almost all of them dressed in orange. They find a spot beside an intensely nervous Indian man and settle themselves on the cold concrete floor. The man introduces himself in a whisper. His name is Arun. He has been in love with Bhagwan since 1969. His mother and father are here too, he says, gesturing to an elderly couple nearby. The couple smile politely. They have followed Bhagwan here, from Bombay. There is no point getting ready, Arun tells them. Nothing can prepare you. Every night, he feels sure he is having a heart attack. Any day now, his heart might explode.

The talking around them dies down and a mood of nervous excitement sweeps across the room. Deep breathing. People's stomachs groaning. The smell of farts. A giggle. The sound of distant traffic. And then, at last, the crunching noise of car wheels on gravel just outside. A sudden energy moves through the crowd, like a wave.

He's here.

And then, finally, he appears.

The Guru.

There is an audible collective gasp. Hushed hysteria. A ripple of spontaneous laughter.

Bhagwan.

He is grinning. He glides into the room in a long white robe that hides his feet. His hands are pressed together in prayer, in greeting, *Namaste.*

People are grabbing the air, rubbing their faces with it. People are weeping. Other people are beaming with happiness.

Look at these dumb cunts, Vincent thinks, but his heart is thumping.

Very carefully, very gracefully, Bhagwan sits down in the waiting chair.

Silence.

He looks around the room, smiling.

Vincent can't help smiling, too.

Bhagwan adjusts the microphone and begins to talk in another language.

'What the hell is he saying? What language is this?'

'Hindi,' Arun whispers. He's talking in Hindi. Next month will be English.

'Shhh,' someone says.

Vincent flashes Kurt a look. *What should we do?*

They don't understand a word of it. But you can't just get up and leave.

Friends, it is not possible to leave before discourse is over: a sign he'd glanced at on the way in.

They're going to have to sit through the whole bloody thing. And how long does it go for? An hour? Two hours? Fuck.

Resigning himself finally, Vincent tries to get comfortable. The floor is cold. His legs are hurting already, sitting like this. His hip. His bum. His ankle. He needs a cigarette. He should have had a piss before they came in. And yet, there is something mesmerising about the guy's voice, he has to admit. He's definitely some kind of hypnotist, the way he uses his hands, his gestures. He's got the tricks. The soft lull of his voice. It's impossible not to be impressed. The voice is speaking. It rises and falls. Beside Vincent, Arun appears to be shivering. Vincent closes his eyes and submits at last. He may as well. He's here now. He understands nothing, and yet he can hear words he recognises among the stream of incomprehensible syllables. Words that are not really there, and that are not even *words*, really. They are sensations in his mind and in his body, too, somehow, a kind of knowledge in his chest.

Do not apologise, he hears.

Everything is perfect.

You do *have a life, and the glory that is streaming from that life is inconceivable.*

He opens his eyes. Blinks. But what is happening? Water is streaming down his face. Vincent is crying. He is crying.

It is early afternoon, the following day, and Vincent is sitting in the ashram garden, trying to meditate. It doesn't come easily. His mind is all over the place. Vivid memories of Astra spiral out into elaborate fantasies. Inevitably, his mind is drawn back to the day she broke up with him. She'd been sleeping with her therapist for months, who she would later cheat on with a film-maker, who she subsequently left for a girl whose name, apparently, was Kristine Kristofferson, and on and on it would go, Vincent suspected. Astra called this incurable dissatisfaction 'fear of the known', and she traced it back to a childhood encounter with UFOs. Of course, it might also have had something to do with being the spoilt youngest daughter of formerly progressive Liberal-voting lawyers, who bailed her out of every problem as a way to pacify their own guilty consciences. 'I'll always love you,' Astra had said. 'You know that, don't you? We're going to be friends forever.' And then they had made love again one last time, even though the sheets were still stained with her therapist's sperm, and, two days later, Vincent had driven out to Daylesford with two bottles of Scotch and a bottle of sleeping tablets. He doesn't remember a lot after that. There was a cheap motel beside the highway. There were brown curtains, and brown carpet. And then there was waking up in the hospital, with doctors and tubes and pins in his leg, and an absolutely unbelievable headache. He shifts his posture. His legs hurt. Then he thinks about Bhagwan, and something that Bhagwan had written. He's been reading a little pamphlet he picked up at the ashram shop. *Just accept everything*, Bhagwan wrote. *Welcome sorrow, just as you welcome happiness*. Easier said than bloody done. Vincent tries to concentrate on his breath, but his mind darts away again, and he is thinking about the house in Byron Street, *his* house, and about Havoc, who is renting it while Vincent is away. He wonders if Havoc has burnt the place down. He wouldn't put it past him. He should call him, find out. He wonders if there's a phone in the ashram, how expensive it will be. He hasn't called home yet. His money situation isn't great. Maybe he could ask Havoc to wire him an advance on the rent. An advance on the advance. Havoc, who has taken more acid than anybody else he knows. He probably should have left someone else in charge. It was irresponsible, he thinks. 'Irresponsible', which is the word his father always used, although he hasn't spoken to his father for almost a year now. 'Typical,' he can hear his father say. And he remembers sitting in church listening to one of his father's interminable sermons, aged thirteen maybe, his father droning on and on, while Vincent sat in the back row and quietly set fire to the hymn book. *Angels from the realms of glory*, blah blah blah, and then the whole little booklet went up in flames! The shrieks of old ladies! The smoke! And the thrashing afterwards. It was weeks before he could sit down properly. And was that the day his father took the dog out to the back paddocks to be shot?

No, that was a different day — he has conflated the two. A yellow-brown kelpie mutt that had been accused of killing the neighbour's chickens, though Vincent was sure it wasn't true. He remembers swimming in the irrigation channel with that dog, who still returns home in dreams sometimes. Digger. A good dog. But he is supposed to be meditating. He comes back to his breath. His stomach rises and falls. The breath on his upper lip. He tries to listen to the stillness in his heart, but he doesn't really know what that means. His mind rushes away like a dog moving from scent to scent. And whatever happened to Kristine Kristofferson?

When he opens his eyes at last, the light is blue and shocking, and the grass in front of him seems imbued with a powerful sense of purpose. Even the strange ants with their big, bulbous heads seem to be teeming with meaning. Soon this feeling passes.

Then he sees Kurt walking towards him. And beside Kurt is a very attractive girl, dressed in orange, with short blonde hair and an exceedingly graceful way of walking. She flows towards him.

'Rani,' Kurt says, 'this is Vince. Another bloody Aussie. My two favourite people in the world.'

Surprised by this statement, Vincent stands and puts his hand out. But Rani goes in for the hug, and he feels her substantial breasts pressing against him through her thin orange dress. Rani is from Sydney originally, with a slight American accent now. She had been in L.A., acting, but now she's here, doing this, with Bhagwan.

'Which is just infinitely — literally — more beautiful.' She laughs brightly.

'Rani is way too smart to be an actor,' Kurt says. 'That's the problem.'

They walk together to the restaurant, an outdoor eating area among trees, behind the office. Rani stops here and there to greet people, to embrace them, to stroke their arms and gaze serenely into their eyes.

'She's just finished the tantra group,' Kurt explains. 'She's in a really powerful space.'

Kurt is clearly very happy. It doesn't matter that Rani has been moving with other people. They are in love again. The Himalayas are off the cards now. Whatever happens with Bhagwan, Kurt is staying. It seems everything is going to be okay, for him. Mark and Mitch, meanwhile, have drifted away with some other Canadians, which is actually for the best. No hard feelings. They are wearing orange already. Vincent sees them sitting on the other side of the courtyard. He waves but doesn't approach them.

Eventually, Rani leads them to a table where a group of attractive sannyasins are finishing their lunch, picking with their hands from metal plates, like naturals. The sound of Spanish, English, Marathi, Japanese, French, German. There are smiles and introductions, a mood of friendliness. Vincent recognises the girl he saw carrying the watermelon on the first day, the one who looked at him, who reminded him of Astra. He manoeuvres himself towards her. Rani introduces them.

'This is Yamini,' Rani says.

Yamini has risen to greet them. She recognises Vincent, flashing again that same mischievous smile.

She does, in fact, look a bit like Astra, he thinks. Although she is taller, it's true, and she has a larger nose, there is something familiar about the way she is squinting at him now, teasingly, the way she seems to be openly assessing him. She has the same waist-length dark hair that Astra had, parted in the middle, and she is wearing a puffy pink blouse beneath an orange vest that he likes. As with everyone else at the table, a string of beads dangles from her neck — a *mala* — with a little black-and-white image of Bhagwan hanging from one end.

'Vincent,' says Vincent. 'G'day.'

Amazingly, they embrace. He can smell her underarms, but it is not unpleasant. It is the opposite of unpleasant.

Yamini is half Italian — 'Roman,' she tells him — but she has lived in London for most of her life. Her mother is English. She has her mother's posh, girlish accent, it seems, and her father's flawless Mediterranean skin.

'Wow,' Vincent says, and 'No,' he's never been to either of those places. This is his first time overseas. 'Straight to India, yeah. Pretty wild. What an amazing country.'

Yamini has been here for three months, she tells him, shaking her head as if she still can't believe it. Not so long ago, she was living in a squat in Hackney, a very heavy political scene. She and her boyfriend left to travel through India. But he was on a real power trip, and they'd split up after three weeks.

Vincent nods understandingly, and silently rejoices.

'I didn't know what I was going to do,' Yamini says. Eventually, she decided to go to Italy to study radical puppetry. Her father lives in Naples. 'In Napoli.' She could have stayed with him. But then she heard about Bhagwan.

'I wasn't looking for a guru,' she says. 'It just happened.'

Already it feels like she is confiding in him.

'And you?' she asks, touching his arm, the skull tattoo. 'You have just arrived today?'

'No,' Vincent says, genuinely hurt. 'No. We got here ... I mean, I saw you ... a couple of days ago.'

'Of course,' she says, although it's clear that she doesn't remember him. She must give the same look to everyone.

'We've got darshan tonight,' Vincent says, recovering, trying to keep things moving between them. 'Bit nervous about that.'

'Oh!' Yamini exclaims, as if this news alone fills her with almost unbearable joy. She reaches out again to touch his chest. Her small brown hand presses against his heart. 'I'm so jealous,' she says.

Sunset. Unreal beauty. Golden light sparkling in the steaming garden. On the other side of the black metal gates, light catches the white edge of Lao Tzu House. Bhagwan's house, where he lives and sleeps.

Vincent and Kurt are waiting in line, with thirty or so other people, for darshan. Soft conversation. A feeling of freshness, of expectation and joy. Everyone cleanly showered. Somewhere, someone is playing a sitar. A woman calmly ticks their names off a list.

Kurt is talking about Rani, about how she has changed.

Yamini, Vincent is thinking. *Yamini. Yamini. Yamini.*

Shoes and Mind are to be left here at the gates, a sign reads.

And then at last, the gates open. Two different women lean in to sniff them, more intimately this time. Vincent can feel their warm breath on his neck. Again, they are allowed to enter. A thickly bearded man gestures along the path. They walk in silence through dense foliage, to another, smaller open-air auditorium. A white-marble building glowing like an apparition in the jungle.

And inside, a single, waiting white chair, around which people arrange themselves in a series of semicircles. Vincent and Kurt are two rows from the back. The marble floor is cool. Through an open doorway Vincent can see into Bhagwan's house. A lighted hallway, bookshelves. A view of illicit intimacy.

They wait in silence for what feels like a long time. Vincent is more nervous than he expected; his heart is pounding in his head. His breath rises and falls. He tries to concentrate and fails. His mind flicks through dozens of topics, but it feels like he is underwater, like he might actually faint.

From somewhere an image comes to him, an old memory: the branches of a huge, drooping tree suddenly lifting from a river. He was a teenager, barely thirteen. At his father's insistence, he had sold his motorbike to a friend of his older brother for ten pounds and a hand-grenade.

But what do you do with a hand-grenade?

Finally, he pulled the pin and threw it into the muddy river.

A tower of water, that's what he remembers now. A weeping willow at the edge of the river. The heavy branches lifting in shock.

And then a kind of electricity sweeps through the audience, a deeper silence. A light goes off and on again inside the house.

Suddenly, Bhagwan appears in the doorway, a figure flooded with light, floating towards them.

Namaste, slowly turning to greet them all. Just like the other day, but so much closer now. Bhagwan is grinning. A look of such kindness. Slowly, he takes his seat.

Vincent has to remember to breathe. He cannot take the smile off his face.

Two women sit cross-legged at Bhagwan's side — one of them the woman they met at the office, Laxmi — together with a tall, serious, red-headed man called Shiva, who is Bhagwan's bodyguard.

Laxmi calls out a name, and someone gets up to sit at Bhagwan's feet.

Three people are called like this, a conversation happens, although from where Vincent is sitting, it's hard to hear everything that is being said.

And then it's Kurt's turn.

Kurt is visibly shaking as he makes his way to the front. Vincent strains forward to listen, but he still feels as if he is underwater. Bhagwan is smiling. Vincent can see the back of Kurt's head, his wild, blonde hair. Kurt is saying something. There is laughter from the audience. Then Bhagwan is speaking to Kurt. It is a long speech. He is talking slowly, very delicately, with a whistly hiss at the end of each *s*, like a trail of smoke.

'Do not think of death as something outside of you,' Bhagwan is saying. 'Death is *not* ... something outside of yourself. And do not think of death ... as something in the future ... it is not. Death is ... within you.' His eyes widen. 'Death ... is the other side of life. In fact, life *is* death. Only covered, does it appear as life.'

Kurt is nodding.

Now something is happening. A short exchange that Vincent can't hear.

Kurt bows his head, and Bhagwan places something around his neck. A mala. Kurt has taken sannyas. Just like that. And now he is making his way back to his seat, and Vincent's name is being called.

'Vincent,' Laxmi says again.

But he doesn't know if he will be able to make it. He doesn't know if he will be able to stand up and actually walk twenty feet to the front of the room.

Somehow he does. People reach out to steady him. People's hands. People's faces beaming.

Now he is actually sitting at Bhagwan's feet, and Bhagwan is looking into his eyes and smiling.

The warmth of that gaze floods him.

'So you have come,' Bhagwan says. 'Very good. I have been waiting, mmm. How are you feeling?'

'Terrified,' Vincent whispers.

A ripple of laughter from those around him.

'Good,' Bhagwan says, gently amused by this. 'It is good. This is exactly how it should be. Because now you are here, and you are going into Nothingness. And it is terrifying to go into Nothingness.'

Vincent nods.

'But this is the journey I have planned for you, mmm,' Bhagwan continues, still smiling. 'It is very frightening for the ego. The ego does not want to be annihilated, mmm. It wants to cling. But Nothingness is your true nature, I'm sorry to say.'

More laughter. Bhagwan's huge, kind eyes, seeing him, seeing right through him.

'If the raindrop could feel such things,' Bhagwan says, 'it too would feel this terror, as it falls into the ocean.'

He pauses now, his elegant hand raised in the air, his thumb and forefinger joined.

'It is falling through darkness.'

His hand quivers.

'Soon it will not be a raindrop anymore, mmm. But there is no need for this raindrop to feel such terror. Soon it will be an ocean. The raindrop can relax. It will disappear. Because this is its nature. So you can relax too, yes? You can feel this dissolving as something that is very good, very natural.' His eyes twinkle, and his eyebrows arch magnificently. 'I am going to help you dissolve. That is why you have come here, mmm?'

Vincent realises he is crying again, lucid tears falling cleanly down his face. 'Yes,' he says.

'Right now, I can see you have so much fear,' Bhagwan says. 'And so much anger, too, yes? Enough anger here to kill a man, I think.'

'It's true,' Vincent sobs.

'Good,' Bhagwan continues, pleasantly. 'Good. So let this be a radical change for you, mmm. Now you can begin to let this anger go. This fear. Because they are the same thing. Sometimes the anger is hiding in the fear. And sometimes the fear is hiding in the anger. But they are both taking their energy from the past, yes? And the past is just smoke in the head. It is nothing.'

He moves his hand, as if brushing something from the air.

'It is like a dream,' he continues. 'Like a nightmare. You want to fight it, but you cannot fight it. You cannot kill a nightmare.' He chuckles. 'It is not possible, mmm. You can fight, but you will never succeed. You can only make a mess out of your bed.'

Laughter.

'You can only realise that it is not real. You can only wake up, mmm. And this is the beginning of a great tenderness. A great love affair. You have been fighting in your sleep for such a long time,' he says, still smiling, though his eyes have become strangely blank, as if there is no one there anymore, no person, just an energy pouring from somewhere. 'I am ready to help you to wake up. I have your new name right here. But will you allow me to help you?'

Vincent nods. 'Yes.' His voice catches in his throat. 'Yes.' His face is wet with tears. This wasn't his plan, to take sannyas so easily, to just hand it all over, all the fear and rage and self-loathing and loneliness. But now, of course, he wants this more than anything. To surrender. He has wanted it all his life, without ever knowing it. The relief is extraordinary. Love pours from this being in front of him. He has come home.

'Good,' Bhagwan says, as he leans forward to place the mala around Vincent's neck. 'This will be your new name. Swami Anand Komalatva. Swami means "master". Anand means "bliss". Komalatva means "tenderness". So let this be the beginning of a great tenderness, an overwhelming tenderness, towards the entire existence.'

And now Bhagwan is pressing his thumb into Vincent's forehead.

There are no thoughts.

There is just the almost unbearable experience of life charging through him.

'Anything else to say?' Bhagwan asks.

A pause.

'I love you, Bhagwan,' Vincent says.

'Yes,' Bhagwan says, chuckling. 'I know.'

The past is just smoke in the head, Bhagwan had said, *it is nothing*. But later, during the six hours of uncontrollable weeping that follows this encounter, Vincent lies on the floor of his hotel room and recalls with remarkable clarity the time his father took him to shoot kangaroos at a place called Katamatite. The memory seems to have risen from nowhere. It was winter. He remembers the wind and the cold, the smell of gun oil and the dazzling sun through the scrubby bush. He was eight years old. His brother was in the hospital with rheumatic fever. They couldn't go near him. Instead, he and his father had gone out together.

This rareness alone was cause for recollection. Having his father all to himself. Also, his father's unusual kindness that day, entrusting him with the power of the rifle: a Lee-Enfield .303, with a beautiful walnut stock, which had belonged to Vincent's grandfather. His father's steady hand at his shoulder, showing him where it would kick.

And then the power that ran through him, echoing across the bush.

The kangaroo, which was greyish, lay breathing in a patch of cleared dirt. One of its legs kept kicking, so that its body turned in a sort of circle and swept the ground with its powerful tail. Its head jerked a few times. Then it grew still. Its wet eye looked up but did not seem to comprehend him when he went to stand above it. There were flies already. And there would be dozens of kangaroos in the years to come, and maybe a hundred rabbits, but this was the first — a memory out of nothing, arriving with the force of a brick. There is nothing that separates him from that kangaroo. That is what he feels. They are the same thing. And weeks later, as Vincent is standing above the German, he will remember that kangaroo again, its blood-soaked fur, as if this death has been running secretly through his entire life.

'Tell me who you are?'

It is three days later, and Vincent is sitting cross-legged in front of a man, a soft-faced blonde sannyasin he has never seen before. They are very close; their knees are touching. This is the enlightenment intensive, the first of three therapy groups that Bhagwan has instructed him to take. There are about thirty other people in the room. Beginners mostly, paired up like this, staring nervously into each other's eyes. Vincent is wishing he was somewhere else. Pretty much anywhere would do.

'Who are you?' the man asks again, louder this time.

He has cold blue eyes, and some sort of accent. Dutch? Swiss? Something like that. Not that Vincent has any idea what either of those accents sound like.

'My name is Komalatva,' Vincent says, and is surprised again by disappointment. The feeling of intense certainty that accompanied his darshan has passed. What is he supposed to do with such an absurd name? *Komalatva*. It's almost impossible to say. He understands that Vincent has to die, so that someone else can be born. Sure. But does it have to be someone called Komalatva? Kurt is now called Abhi — just like Abbie Hoffman — which is typical of Kurt. Everything works out for him. Kurt is the sort of person who always gets what he wants. But Komalatva? Komal? Kommie? Koma? There's nothing to be done with it. He knows that this is just one of Bhagwan's provocations, giving him a name so ridiculous that he will have to learn to laugh at himself, along with everyone else. His job is to remain nameless behind this new name, to drop his attachment to his conditional self. Bhagwan said something like that. Still. He is in a foul mood now.

There is also the fact that Kurt has moved in with Rani, which means that Vincent will have to find somewhere else to live. At twenty rupees a day, he can't afford the hotel by himself, certainly not for long. Plus, the phone had cut out before he could speak to Havoc back home to ask for money. He'd waited almost four hours in a little concrete room. But someone else had answered the phone, some bloke he didn't recognise, and then the line had gone dead. A monkey had chewed through a cord, apparently. Worst of all, though, is the fact that he does not know what is happening with Yamini. If *anything* is happening with Yamini. Two days ago, it had felt like they'd really connected. But her coolness, when he ran into her this morning after dynamic meditation, had unsettled him. She had regarded him for a moment as if he were a stranger, with arrogant indifference.

'I might see you later,' she'd said casually, before drifting away with the departing crowd.

But they had not discussed when later would be, and he hadn't been able to find her. Now he was in here, and it would be three days before he saw her again. A lifetime.

The blonde man is still looking at him, expectantly.

'Komal,' Vincent says. 'I am Komal. I'm from Australia. I'm a social worker. I was, I mean. I'm unemployed at the moment. I'm … I'm just trying to figure this all out, you know. I guess I don't really know what the fuck I'm doing here.'

He talks like this for five minutes, avoiding anything of consequence, he realises, even as he is saying it. He is simply filling the silence.

Then a bell rings, and they exchange roles.

'Tell me who *you* are,' Komal says, with considerable relief.

And the man tells him, or tries to, fumblingly, in his imperfect English.

'I am Kuteer,' he says. 'I am twenty-four. I am sorry because my English. I am student in engineering. I am coming here one month. Sometimes I think I will stay and be forever. Sometime I think, no way, you are crazy. I don't know what is to be done. My mother is dying at home in Denmark. She is very religious person. I want to go and be with her and also I don't want to do that. I want to just be here, in this present moment. But always when I am meditating, I am thinking of her dying, without me.'

They do this, back and forth, for forty minutes, and then they find new partners, and begin again.

Komal's next partner is a woman from Essex who was adopted as a child and is very angry about it. She has a sullen, disappointed face and is sweating heavily. Then there's a man from London whose first wife had a miscarriage and left him — he still can't quite believe it, he says. Then there is a woman from New York who tells him that she used to vomit after eating, but would love nothing more now than a cream cheese bagel. It is all she dreams about, she says. Then there is another woman from England, a semi-famous dancer, then a woman from California who has left behind three children to come here. Then a man from Tokyo who speaks almost no English, then a man from New Zealand who was a junkie and a jewellery thief, then another man from Austria who is filled with rage, who hates Jews and queers, then a Spanish woman who says almost nothing, who simply laughs and laughs, then a man from Mexico who lost his whole family in a boating accident and growls in pain. It goes on like this for fourteen hours. Food is brought to them, and they eat in silence. Then a bell rings and they begin again. The pain in his legs, in his back. Words, words, words. The bones of his bum have moved beyond numbness into agony. His skin crawls with an almost unbearable desire to get up and run away. The room is full of flies.

The next person arrives.

'Tell me who you are?' Komal says automatically.

But it doesn't matter by this stage who anyone is. Not for Komal or Vincent or whoever he is supposed to be now. There's just the chaos of the self, as if every part of him were splitting in half, then dividing again and again, into infinity.

Another bell rings. Finally, it's over. It's past midnight. They've done it. Only two more days to go.

Bewildered, exhausted, everyone wanders out of the room, trudges in silence to the communal bathroom. There are no doors. People shit and shower in front of one another. No one has anything else to say. They are just bodies doing their business, like stupefied animals. They will sleep in the ashram tonight, on coconut mats, shut off from everyone else. They will dream their delirious, repetitive dreams, their nightmares of psychic disintegration. They will be woken at 5.30am for dynamic meditation. Then another day of *Who am I?*. Another fourteen fucking hours.

Komal needs a cigarette. He will have to go out the back gate and into the street to smoke. He should feel relief to be outside, but he doesn't. The night is huge and overwhelming. He feels as if a lid has been taken off the earth and he has been exposed to the void beyond, which seems to be crushing his head. He can hear monkeys. He can hear people fucking loudly. Assailed by a loneliness that is close to panic, he walks through the ashram, which is almost empty now. If only he had the Monaro. If only he could drive and drive and never stop. At the gate, Sant, the guard, a tall Indian Sikh, glances at him calmly as he lets him out into the quiet backstreet. Komal lights a cigarette, breathes smoke, looks up at the trees that reach down towards him and from which grey lizards keep plopping onto the road. One of them, seeing him, or seeing him and seeming to understand suddenly what he is, arches its back as if to pounce, before releasing its breath and darting into the bushes.

Either I will commit suicide, Komal thinks, *or something else will have to happen to break the hell of being myself once and for all.*

On the third day, before lunch, he begins to vomit. The group leader, a large, abrasive, intelligent Dutch woman, helps him to stand and leads him to the edge of the room where a tall mirror rests against the wall. The taste of vomit is in his mouth. The smell of it is in the air. Flies come to feed off him. He is handed a tin bowl.

'And continue,' the group leader tells him, pointing at the mirror. 'Don't run away.'

Some people around him are still talking, still describing themselves. 'How does life fulfil itself?' he hears someone ask. 'How does life fulfil itself?'

There is no answer.

The words have lost their meaning.

'Fuck, goddamn it,' someone else says. 'I want fucking pork noodle.'

Others are moaning or wailing. Some are sitting in silence. One is laughing hysterically.

Komal is still now. The nausea has passed. His orange T-shirt, his orange pants are stained with bile and sweat. He feels the deep sadness of the earth like a weight pressing on his shoulders, on his neck. The sadness of humans in their wretchedness. At the same time, he feels a kind of lightness rising through him. He feels the animal strength of his heart beating, the weird miracle of his breath. The way air becomes breath and breath becomes air. A sense of borderlessness. Waves of light and exhaustion bathe everything. Grief and wonder are the same thing. Exhaustion and beauty are the same thing. Snot, blood, vomit, saliva — all the same. Rivers flow with blood, mothers weep for their dead children, and even this is inseparable from the glory. He sees the self in the mirror that he has been trying so hard to protect and to run away from — a terrified child, a terrified teenager, like a mask or a precious statue. A powerful wave of compassion unfolds within him. Behind the mask there is nothing. His body is empty. His skin is empty. His face is empty. His organs are empty. His name is empty. There is nothing behind his name. There is just speechless, unbearable Truth at the centre of everything.

It has been a few days since he finished the enlightenment intensive. Something has changed, there's no doubt about it. He feels lighter. He feels pretty good. Also, Abhi has decided that K is a better name than Komal. So K it is. About this, too, K feels happier, lighter.

In the city, K and Abhi hire motorbikes, and then, together with Rani and Yamini, they ride out to the Karla Caves at Lonavala. It takes two hours, stopping here and there.

Between K and Yamini nothing official has happened, but there is a definite playfulness to Yamini's manner now that gives K hope. And yet it is hard to imagine actually sleeping with her. It would be like embracing a sculpture. And now she is pressed into him on the back of the motorbike, and her arms are wrapped around him.

It is a relief to be away from the ashram for a while, too, to be in the world again, speeding through Indian villages, past goats, chickens, children, crows with their mouths open in the heat. He thinks, *As soon as I get off this motorbike I will get down on my hands and knees and kiss the ground.*

My India, he thinks.

Workers stand in the fields to watch them pass — two orange flashes blasting through the countryside.

The day is hot and the caves, when they finally get there, astonish them. A Buddhist prayer hall, like a giant ribcage carved from the mountain itself more than two thousand years ago. They walk slowly uphill, sweating. On the path leading up the mountain, a man missing half an arm is sweeping. He begs by cupping the elbow of his mutilated arm in his remaining hand.

At the top of the hill, at the entrance to the prayer hall, Rani makes them stop so she can take a photo of each of them standing there. She has bought a camera from an Israeli sannyasin, and her plan is to fund her trip by taking photographs of mountains and temples, which she can sell to publications in the United States. If it weren't for her visa expiring, she'd never have to leave India again, she says.

There is a waterfall nearby, and all four of them take off their clothes and stand naked beneath the rushing water, until they are discovered by a group of local boys. Then they hurriedly dress again and sit down to eat lunch on the rocks. They unwrap the greasy parcels and eat hungrily, Indian pastries, daubs of sticky rice, Indian sweets dripping with honey, warm cola.

The boys approach them. Five intense little kids carrying big sticks. Their oversized trousers drag in the dust. 'Money,' the boys say, seriously. 'Hello money.'

Rani thinks she recognises the tallest of the boys from the burning Ghats. She could have sworn she saw him talking to the Ghat Keeper, a kind of madman who guards the ashes in the days after a burning. But surely that's impossible — the Ghats at Poona are two hours' drive from here, and the boy doesn't respond when she proposes the coincidence. They give the boys a handful of rupees, enough to make them retreat to a nearby rock, where they sit and laugh at the foreigners in their matching orange clothes.

K lights a beedi. Yamini leans into him, resting her head against his shoulder in a way that may or may not be simply friendly, sisterly. The air off the water is cool. They talk about the ashram, gossip mostly. Who is working where. Who has been sent back to the West. Who is moving with who. The way the energy of the place is like a beautiful drug. How beautiful it is that the women are in charge. Laxmi, Mukta, Maneesha, and Deeksha, that dragon in the kitchen.

They are building the future of the world, they agree. The future of humanity.

Above them, bright, unfolding clouds.

Abhi talks about his darshan, his meeting with Bhagwan. 'I was looking into his eyes,' he says, 'and I just knew that I was fucked.'

'I start crying every time I think about him,' Rani says. 'I mean look at me, it's happening again.'

She wipes her eyes, laughing.

K and Rani are booked in to do the rebirth group in three days' time. 'What about rebirth?' K says, addressing Yamini. 'What's it like?'

Yamini tells them about her experience. It was a few weeks ago now. 'I felt like I was going to die,' she says, 'like really. I was totally suffocating.'

K brushes the flies protectively from her face while she speaks in her lovely English voice. Yamini is twenty-two years old, but her first boyfriend died of a heroin overdose when she was sixteen, and there is something hard and distant that comes over her sometimes, and which makes her seem older when it does. This is one of those times.

'I heard this horrible shrieking,' Yamini says, 'and my mind was like: *who is that bitch?* But then I realised it was me. It was me screaming, and all this air was suddenly rushing into me. And then it was just these waves of total bliss, you know, like I could really open myself to life.'

The others nod.

'But you know, I just really got in touch with my mother's sadness,' she continues. 'It's like what Bhagwan said. If you can build a bridge to your mother, then you have the whole earth beneath you, holding you. It's like you've got roots into the world.'

Her mother, Yamini explains, doesn't know how to love anything. 'She was so lonely when I was born,' she says. 'Even before my father left. I had to get away from that emotional cruelty. But now I feel like, if I saw her again, you know, we could almost be friends.'

With her eyes still closed, Yamini raises her thin brown wrist towards K, a gesture of easy familiarity. He passes the little cigarette to her, and their fingers touch. In that instant he knows what will happen: that she wants him, too, that they will be together, that everything will be okay. He is in love. The past is just smoke in the head. It's nothing. He sees himself living like this forever: free, unselfconscious, like a Zen monk or some sort of ancient hunter. Alive and at home in the world, at last.

The sun is like a hand cupping his face.

Later that afternoon, exhausted and sunburnt from the ride home, Yamini and K climb the broken steps of The Celestial Lake. The room is K's. He still hasn't found anything cheaper, or longer term. His funds are running low.

Yamini enters the room ahead of him, and K is conscious now of how filthy it actually is. The dirty marks across the walls reappear, the dead insects he has stopped seeing. He closes the door behind them. On the wall there is the photo of Bhagwan, which has drawn Yamini's attention. She stands beneath it looking up, and then, without saying anything she pulls her long dress over her head and turns around. Naked except for her mala. K can't quite believe it's happening, even though, of course, he knew it would. They move over to the thin bed. He loves the freckles at the edge of her nose. He loves her nose and the bones in her shoulders and her arms and her mouth and her teeth and everything else. He kisses a rash of salty welts along her thighs where the mosquitoes have bitten her. He licks each one, until she pulls him up, impatiently, directing him. And then, quickly and quite suddenly, she comes. It seems as if it has nothing to do with him. Her eyes are closed, and her head is twisted away. Isn't the idea to fuck for hours, in a state of ecstatic meditation? But then he is coming too, he can't help himself. He withdraws messily. Maybe just in time. Or maybe not.

He is kneeling above her, awkwardly. Not exactly tantric, he almost says, but doesn't.

'You're on the pill, aren't you?' he asks instead. A terrible question, badly timed. Anyway, of course she is.

'No,' she says. 'I'm not.'

'Really?'

'No. But it doesn't matter. I've had the knot,' she says.

It takes him a few seconds to realise what she's talking about. She's been sterilised. It's something Bhagwan encourages. The procedure is offered free in the medical centre. *Of course*. Much better than all those abortions, she assures him.

K flops down beside her. Morosely he kisses her neck. He puts his lips to her earlobe. He is thinking for some reason, about one of

Yamini's other lovers, Dasana, who is in the health clinic, recovering from hepatitis. Dasana, with his fantastic Italian cock and immense inheritance from his family's industrial fertiliser company.

'Mmm, that was nice,' Yamini says at last.

Was it? K can't think of what to say.

From outside, in the stench and heat of the afternoon, they can hear the deep rattle of rickshaws, the sound of yelling and drilling. An old woman is calling out a single repetitive sentence.

'She's selling bananas,' K says.

'What?'

'The woman. Outside.'

'Oh,' Yamini laughs.

They listen together.

It is a beautiful sound now, which has returned them to each other.

'How long have you and Abhi known each other?' Yamini asks after a while.

'Abhi?' he says. 'Not long. Why?'

'He loves you, you know?'

'What do you mean?'

'Nothing. Just that. He just thinks you're fantastic. He's very protective of you.'

But why? K wonders. He can't understand it, although he recognises that she's right.

He traces the thin bones in her hand.

Then she takes her hand away, and, with her bitten fingernails, lazily strokes the tattoo on his left arm: the skull with the knife through it.

'I love this,' she says.

'Really?' He was twelve when he got these tattoos. And for three years he kept them hidden from his parents.

They have not talked much yet about their families. They have not talked much about anything, except for the ashram itself.

Yamini is the youngest of three sisters, she tells him now. Her parents separated when she was eleven. Her father moved back to Italy. It was terrible, she says. Everything collapsed. Her father is a diplomat, and she clearly still adores him. He sends her money. 'I'm his favourite,' she says, 'and that's the reason my mother has never forgiven me.'

K thinks about them both, she and him, living their strange, hostile childhoods on opposite sides of the world, oblivious of each other and yet destined, somehow, to be together.

'I think we're both misfits,' Yamini says, climbing onto him again. 'But this is where we belong now. I can't imagine anything else.' Her hot breath flutters against his eyelashes. 'This is the real thing,' she whispers.

The shadows creep across the room. The light is the colour of burnished copper through the tattered curtains. Bhagwan looks down on them from his wooden frame.

What have I done to deserve this much happiness? K thinks, and for a moment, for longer than a moment, his love for Yamini and his love for Bhagwan are indistinguishable.

K does the rebirth group and feels what it's like to be born again. He crumples himself into a ball, tighter and tighter. He feels life surging relentlessly through him. He pushes himself through mounds of sweaty pillows. Hands reach for him. People take hold of him by the shoulders. He can feel himself being dragged out into the world.

The air rushes into his lungs as if for the first time. He lies naked on the ground, panting, crying. He remembers what it felt like — to be unwanted almost immediately. His mother's cold gaze. He looks up and sees Bhagwan's face smiling down from a photograph on the wall. It is the face of immense, unconditional love. Rani is there, too, guiding him. They are both naked. She strokes his face while he weeps.

There is no shame.

K loves India now. The smells. The sounds. The chaos. Life in all its aspects. He is in love with the richness of the world. Things that were inconceivable two months ago have become possible. Everything he was is different, stranger, more natural. The span of his life seems epic now. Each day is a new beginning. Every morning, he gets down on his hands and knees and kisses the dust, and at night, in the damp heat, he sings and dances for hours in Buddha Hall. K has never liked dancing that much. He's always been too self-conscious, though he likes being stoned and listening to music. He likes Hank Williams, the Delta blues, Big Joe Turner. He likes AC/DC and The Rolling Stones and Hawkwind. Now, amid hundreds of sweating bodies, in mindless bliss, he twirls and weeps to the ashram music group. *Glory to you Bhagwan*, he sings, again and again and again. *You're a fountain of love, of love. You're a river of love, of love. You're an ocean. Hallelujah.*

Finally, he gets onto Havoc, back home. The connection is terrible.

'Mate,' he yells, 'it's Vince,' and already the name sounds wrong in his mouth.

'Vince! Fucking hell, mate, what's going on?'

'I couldn't explain it if I tried,' K says. 'And you wouldn't believe it anyway. It's the biggest contradiction of my life. I'm fucked. I'm totally fucked, mate. It's amazing.'

The house has not burnt down, after all. Everything is fine. But Australia, Melbourne, Byron Street. It's all so far away, and so ordinary. The phone line crackles. He cannot conceive of ever walking those streets again.

K has moved into a tiny room on the first floor of a villa not far from the ashram, the former residence of British army officers. He has struck a six-month deal. There are bars on the windows and almost nothing in it but light. He strings thin orange curtains. He scrubs the filthy walls, and hangs the picture of Bhagwan from a high nail in the corner. The next day, on a whim, he buys a dozen bluestone boulders from a building site on the corner and pays a teenage boy to help him carry them up the stairs, one by one. He makes an ornamental garden beneath Bhagwan's portrait, a little stone altar, from which potted ferns and frangipanis are soon growing. This feels like an act of commitment: to carry stones and lay them here, to use his hands to pray. Two days later, Yamini visits for the first time.

They climb the steps of the villa together as large green beetles or ants drop from the overhanging trees.

'But what are they?' Yamini says excitedly, squatting to inspect them.

They have the heads of huge ants and the green bodies of beetles, and they appear to be drunk or dying. They writhe in their thousands on the concrete balcony outside the door.

K unlocks the big bolt, and Yamini, leaping over the insects, enters the room and twirls.

'We're like adventure-book siblings, you and I,' she says, giddy with the novelty of a new place.

Siblings? K thinks. *In a children's book?*

But they do make love, eventually.

'I've had too much sex to be interested in a love affair,' Yamini says afterwards. They are lying beside each other.

'What do you mean?' he asks, trying not to appear alarmed.

She turns to look into his eyes. 'What I mean is, I'm ready for something else.'

'Okay. Like … what, exactly?'

'I want your soul, you idiot,' she laughs. 'I want to eat it up.'

They agree that Yamini will move in when K finishes his third therapy group, the *tathata* encounter, which begins in a week.

Later, at The Blue Diamond, they drink cold beer. Then they go out and run through the dark streets. People watch them. They are crazy westerners, crazy with happiness. It is wonderful to drink beer, to be drunk and to run through the streets of a strange city, while people stand and stare. To be in love with everything. To fall over and get up again, laughing and bleeding. They are like angels, like moths beating against the doors of paradise. That's what it feels like, to them.

K has been in Poona for almost two months when he begins Anala's tathata encounter, which is held in a musty, padded room beneath the ashram. As usual, K is early. The floor is covered with mattresses, there are no windows, and the light is dim. Even still, K can make out murky stains on the walls.

An exhausted-looking older woman is already here, sweating

profusely. She has a round face and short, greying hair, and she does not acknowledge K's presence. Instead, she stands gazing at her own feet, humming nervously to herself, like a crazy person. Gradually, others arrive. Nine women and, including K, nine men, all dressed in orange. They introduce themselves. A tall Swedish woman called Veena, who K recognises from the rebirth group, a French man with a sallow face, an American called Devam, who he has met before through Abhi, a stern Australian woman from Adelaide who has just arrived and seems almost sick with fear. Another American guy, an ex-marine called Vikram, huge and taciturn, paces off to one side, while a pretty German woman and a skinny German man exchange sharp, conspiratorial sentences. The others are Dutch, American, Swiss, Japanese, English. These are the people he is going to spend the next five days with. There are no Indians. Indians are not allowed to do group. It is the westerners who need therapy, apparently, who need to learn how to surrender.

Soft voices. Nervous laughter. People agree the ashram is beautiful, like nothing they have ever known. There is a rumour about a man whose nose was broken in last month's tathata group.

'It's true,' K says. 'I know him.' It was Abhi.

'Shit gets brutal,' Devam says sagely. Devam has done his fair share of psychotherapy back in the States: Reichian bodywork, Gestalt, primal scream.

Anala, the group leader, whose name means God of fire, is a sunburnt, heavily bearded, balding Californian. He is carrying a tape player, which he connects to a power point in a corner of the room and loads with a cassette. Soft flute music plays. When he is satisfied, he turns to the room and instructs everyone to sit in a circle.

Ceremoniously taking his own place, Anala looks each of them in the eye, one after the other.

A long silence follows.

Finally, with an air of apparent disappointment, Anala begins to speak.

'Guys,' he says, 'everyone here is totally fucked up.'

'Too right,' someone says. It's Devam.

'You, Devam, especially, because you think you know what's going on.'

'Thank you.'

'Sometimes, you've gotta make some decisions,' Anala continues. 'Your boat is too heavy. You gotta chuck some shit overboard. So that's what we're gonna be doing in here for the next five days. Shit is gonna get pretty heavy. We're gonna have to make some decisions about what's dragging us down, as human beings. What are we gonna chuck overboard? What are we gonna drop?'

He looks from face to face.

'There's only three rules in here,' he says. 'Rule One: don't attack me. Rule Two: ask permission to use the toilet. Rule Three: just keep the energy moving. Beyond that, everything is yours. Just be total. And what that means is, I want you to think of yourself as the first man, the first woman. You don't know anything yet. You don't know anyone. There are no priests. No mommies and daddies. No babysitters. No limits. Nobody has told you how to be. You gotta find out for yourself how to be. And the way to do that is just by accepting whatever comes up. That's what tathata means. It means *suchness*. It's the *is*-ness of whatever *is*, you know what I'm saying? If you're angry, go with the anger. If you're horny, feel that energy. If you wanna cry,

I wanna hear you cry like a fucking baby.'

A long silence.

Nothing happens.

No one wants to make the first move. Time drags on.

Someone sighs heavily.

Veena, the Swedish girl, giggles.

Vikram, the ex-marine, is clearly not having a good time. His face has turned red, the veins in his neck are swollen. He is clenching and unclenching his fists.

Now something is going to happen. K can feel it.

'Hey man,' says Devam, getting up and going over to sit in front of Vikram. 'You wanna do something?'

Vikram stares at him for what seems like an incredibly long time. At last, he opens his mouth. 'Do you wanna die?' he says flatly.

'Nah, man, I just mean, why don't you move your energy or something?'

Vikram stands up. Before anyone can figure out what's going to happen, he has picked Devam up and thrown him against the wall.

All at once the group pounces on Vikram. They pull him to the floor, struggling to hold him down, while he thrashes, screaming. 'I'm gonna kill that fucking cunt!'

K has Vikram's huge right arm pinned to the mattress. He is using all his strength just to hold it there. The German guy has the other arm. The Japanese man has thrown himself across Vikram's chest. Others are struggling to hold his legs. The old woman has been kicked in the face. Blood is flowing from her nose, and she seems to be crying. Meanwhile, the woman from Adelaide has begun to scream. It is a very high-pitched sound. She stops to take a breath and begins again. Anala hasn't moved. He looks thoroughly unfazed. Vikram writhes and spits. 'I'm gonna murder that motherfucker.'

Then his eyes close and he goes quiet.

Everyone waits. Is it a trick?

Slowly, K releases his grip. Nothing.

Vikram has passed out.

Stunned silence. Devam is shaking. The old woman is moaning in the corner of the room. She is sucking her thumb like a child.

Time passes. K doesn't know how long. Five minutes? Ten? Boredom takes over.

People sit slumped around the enormous figure. What has happened?

Finally, Vikram opens his eyes.

'What happened?' he says. His voice is soft, bewildered, like a child's. And then, almost silently, he begins to cry.

Veena strokes his head. Carefully, they all come over to him again. They form a circle, lay their hands on him, take turns to wipe the snot and tears from his face. Someone begins to hum, to chant. Vikram's eyes are the eyes of a baby. Even Devam is here now, sitting beside his attacker, his own eyes closed. K is between a French woman and the tall German man. He takes Vikram's hand in his own. Now they are all swaying back and forth and everyone is chanting. Someone turns up the volume on the music. Drumming sounds. Flute. When K opens his eyes again, he sees that the circle is disintegrating. People are standing around, swinging their arms. Some are lurching spastically. The music quickens. Vikram is on his feet, swaying gently back and forth. The music changes again. People begin to dance. Veena is taking off her clothes. Then the German woman disrobes. Then Devam begins stepping awkwardly from his pants. Eventually, K undresses, too. Soon even the old lady is naked, her large breasts swinging. Her face is still smeared with blood, but her nose has stopped bleeding. K is dancing alongside the German woman. He's forgotten her name. She has a look of rapture on her face. Bodies. Music. Exhalation. Gratitude. Boredom. Love. It goes on and on and on. 'I'm here to chop off your head,' Bhagwan said. K thinks of Yamini, carrying a watermelon, like a severed head, like an omen. People begin to fall to the ground, exhausted. At some point they begin moving over the top of one another, a blind mass, and K has his face pressed between someone's thighs. It's difficult to breathe. Something is sticking into his leg. Someone's cock. He takes it in his hand and begins stroking it. There are breasts in his face. Large, purple nipples. He begins sucking. The taste of blood. It's the old woman. She is old enough to be his grandmother. She is saying something, but it's not a word, as far as he can tell. People are moaning, writhing. There is the mindlessness of flesh, the thick smell of bodies, of sweat and sperm. It's almost impossible to tell who is who, and it doesn't matter anyway.

Late in the afternoon on the third day, something else happens. They are all sitting on the floor, naked. They have been watching an English woman fuck the Japanese man, so that her husband, an English guy, can appreciate the desperate tenacity of his own attachments. The air is soupy, pungent, almost revolting. A fly has gotten in. Everyone is in a bad mood. The fly moves invisibly from person to person, throwing each of them in turn into a spasm of irritation.

A long silence, while Anala stares hard at each person.

K swats at the fly.

'Now,' Anala says at last. 'I'm gonna tell you all what your trip is. Because there are some serious fucking head-cases in this room. Starting with you, Veena.'

'What the fuck?' the Swedish woman says.

'Come on, you can do better than that.'

'You misogynist fuck,' she says. 'You fucking power-tripping pig-shit-eating fucking dick-hole—'

'Yeah! So much anger. Let it out. That's great. Devam, why don't *you* tell Veena what you think of her?'

Devam moves over to Veena and screams into her face, a long howl, which throws her into a fresh rage. She spits in his face and begins pounding him around the ears. He slaps her. She slaps him back. She claws at him with her fingernails, drawing blood. She is screaming in a mixture of Swedish and English now, something about men, something about their miserable, godforsaken cocks.

Encouraged by this atmosphere, small fights begin to erupt around the room. Anala moves among them, whispering to them, urging them on. They need to get this aggression out, he tells them. It's poisoning them all.

'This is what we're holding, inside us,' he says. 'Get to know it.'

He comes over to K and speaks into his face, a hissing sound. The words are lost in the noise of the room.

'What?' K says.

'You're not into it, man,' Anala says again. 'Have you come here just to waste our fucking time? Why don't you run back to your mommy? Why don't you run back to your little daddy if you don't want to get involved.'

The rage is sudden and dark, something volcanic spitting up from deep within him.

'Not at me, man,' Anala says, reeling backwards. 'Give it to *him*.' He ducks behind the tall German man.

Caught off guard, K doesn't know what to do. But then the German man steps forward and shoves him, a jolt that sends him staggering backwards.

'Verflucht noch mal,' the German says, lifting his chin in a gesture of arrogant dismissal. 'Du scheisse, du scheisse.'

Hans. That's the man's name. But K is not thinking about him. He is thinking about someone else, another German man called Mr Sugar, who was a friend of his father's. When he was seven years old, K and his brother were sent to live with Mr Sugar on a farm, far out in the country somewhere.

Over the years, the events of those two months have slipped further and further from K's conscious mind. He recalls Mr Sugar's very beautiful gun more often than he does the tortures that were inflicted on him. In dreams, occasionally, or caught in the smells of certain foods — cabbage or mashed potatoes — K will intuit some flicker of memory. The house in the country. The fizz of spider webs in a type of forest. The old copper, where Mr Sugar's wife washed clothes. A dirt floor. Sometimes he feels something like a belt pinch at his wrist, where Mr Sugar used to tie his hands behind his back. 'Eat,' Mr Sugar would say, and K would have to eat from the bowl like a dog. Even after he had vomited his food back into his own plate, he was obliged to finish everything. He was obliged to lick the plate clean to show his gratitude.

But there is something else too that intercedes now, as Hans comes towards K, with his long face distorted by his own incomprehensible hatreds. It is the muscle memory from K's time in a cold boxing gym in Footscray. He was a teenager then, a gangly southpaw. Not a particularly good boxer. A smart-arse. The trainer had disliked him, and would set him up to get beaten by much bigger kids. And yet the knowledge of that old way of moving is still present in his body, and it returns now, as the German comes towards him. Feinting left, K snaps forward and hits him with a hard jab to the nose. There is a strange popping sound, and the man stops, surprised. He opens his mouth, which is filled with blood and lifts his hand towards his face as K hits him again, a left hook to the side of the chin. The German topples. It has taken less than five seconds, and if they really were in a ring, with rules, it would all be over now. K is off-balance, and there is no need to throw another punch. But there are no rules, and K falls, and lands on the man with his knees, and continues punching. The desire to kill is a powerful freedom. He does not know, nor will he ever know, how long this goes on for. Mere seconds, perhaps. Or many seconds. Then someone is dragging him backwards, and now he is standing again, as he once stood looking down at a kangaroo, many years earlier. The memory flashes through him. And there are flies here as well, and someone brushes them away from the soggy bowl that is the German man's face.

K is standing by himself with his back to the padded wall.

Hans has been taken away, carried out the back gate of the ashram by four men, by Devam and Vikram and two others, and down the street to the ashram's medical centre. Beyond that, it is not clear, to anyone, what has happened. If Hans is even alive.

'Will he be okay?' the Australian woman asks.

'He was breathing,' Veena says.

'Of course he was breathing,' Anala assures her. 'Everything will be fine.' He dismisses the group. The day is nearly done anyway.

'Do we come back?' someone asks. There are still two days to go.

'Of course,' Anala says. 'The circus goes on.' He slaps K on the back. 'Get some sleep, buddy,' he says. 'Take it easy.'

When K emerges into the dusk, the air is blissfully cool after the stuffiness of the bunker. It is the middle of darshan, and the rest of the ashram is quiet at this hour. He walks out though the main gate and into the street, confused. The smell of damp soil, of exhaust fumes. The sweetness of rotting fruit.

Thinking back afterwards, he will remember certain things about the next few hours: a numb rickshaw ride back to the villa, and then a long walk through dirty, darkened, tree-lined streets, past fires, and bony cows, and figures huddled in the darkness. There will be pigs and faces, and, at one point, a group of boys, who will follow him, fighting among themselves as they try to persuade him of something. He will ignore them until they fall behind. He will remember tripping and hurting his hand and getting up. He will remember eating on a street corner, in a part of the city he has never seen before, eating and soon afterwards vomiting, and then wandering off again until, entirely by accident, he finds himself among the recognisable shapes of his own neighbourhood. He will remember climbing the stone steps and the thin bed and a sense of unendurable time, hours spent staring at the ceiling, the walls, the fan. There will be unreal, swirling images, dreams that aren't dreams. And from high up in the corner, Bhagwan's portrait will stare down at him with that same smile, which strikes him, suddenly, as indifferent.

K does not return to the bunker on the fourth day. He sleeps fitfully instead, and leaves his room only once, to eat an oily pancake on the corner in the late afternoon. Light falls through the mango trees and softens the dusty air. He should go to the medical centre, he knows. He should see if Hans is alright. But he doesn't. Nearby, an old woman is squatting at a roadside fire, boiling water. She has been collecting dry weeds, and now she is breaking sticks and adding them to the flames. Watching her, a kind of tranquillised calm overtakes him. An almost blissful acceptance of the world. A dog dozes beside him in the shade of an old Enfield. Eventually, he makes his way back to his room. Lying on his bed again, he has a distant memory of being sick as a child, of staying home from school. Tiny spiders like flowers drop from the ceiling above him. There is the rattle of motorbikes or rickshaws, the sounds of the day fading, the sounds of the night coming on. There is the feeling, increasingly powerful, but not unpleasant, that he does not exist.

But Hans is not at the medical centre, when K finally summons the courage to visit the next day. He has been transferred to the hospital, an Iranian physician tells him. He is alive. He has been badly beaten. His nose has been broken. He has at least three cracked ribs and severe concussion. There is very likely internal bleeding. 'Did you see what happened?' the doctor asks, quietly, as if it is a secret.

'No,' says K, already leaving. 'No. But thanks.'

He takes a rickshaw to the hospital, a dusty three-storey building about fifteen minutes away. It is alarmingly crowded, and he has a hard time even finding someone he can ask a question of. He is directed to the third floor, then to the second, then back to the third. The hallways have begun to seem familiar, certain marks on the stairs, certain faces. In a rising panic, he sits for more than an hour on a bench in a small green room, while a steady mass of wounded and dying people exchange places around him. It is unclear exactly what he is waiting for and he leaves before his name is called — if that indeed was ever going to happen — without finding Hans, and returns to the villa. He tries to meditate but can't. He cannot shake the feeling that he has failed, and that this failure has something to do with his own nature.

For more than a week there is no news of Hans, although he is not well-known around the ashram, it turns out.

According to Anala, Hans was discharged from the hospital two days after he was admitted, but no one has seen him since. Maybe he's gone to Bombay, where the opium and the heroin are cheaper. Or maybe he's just lying low, recovering.

K's fear is that he will run into Hans at any moment. And yet, a part of him wills this, too, the moment of confrontation and — he hopes — of redemption and forgiveness. A number of times over the following days, he thinks he sees Hans from afar: in line for discourse, getting out of a rickshaw at the front gate. The moment is almost on him when he realises his mistake. It's always someone else.

There are rumours, too. A man has thrown himself from the fifth floor of a nearby apartment block. But when? The details are sketchy. A sannyasin, almost certainly. But an American? A European? There's nothing official. Meanwhile, the naked corpse of an unidentified male westerner has been found in the mud near the river. Murdered by locals, is the story. The body was taken to the hospital morgue, but the power in the morgue failed, apparently., and the corpse had to be disposed of before a proper autopsy could be conducted.

His name?

But no one knows.

Could *that* have been Hans? It's impossible to say. There are thousands of sannyasins, coming and going. Many of them live in straw huts at the edge of the river, or in fields. There's no way to keep track of everyone.

And there's no reason to assume the worst, Abhi tells him.

Exactly. Everything is going to be alright, he decides. And why shouldn't it be? After all, the whole thing was Bhagwan's idea. That they should unleash their own raw selves upon each other. That was the plan, wasn't it? All he did was do what he was told to do. Surrender.

Slowly, the intensity of K's shame fades. Hans is, no doubt, fine. He's probably just licking his wounds somewhere. It doesn't matter so much now, either, that K never finished the encounter group, that he walked out of the operation before he could be stitched back up. *It is what it is*, he tells himself. He allows the loving energy of the ashram to welcome him back, as if from a long, confusing journey. It is Christmas, weirdly. And then it is the New Year. It is 1977, the future. The memories from those underground days, already strangely unreal, begin to recede. Best of all, Yamini has moved into his room at last. Their love, K feels, is transforming him. Already he recognises a new gentleness in himself, a freshness. They are learning, bit by bit, to play and fight and laugh together, without clinging to some rigid idea of themselves, or each other.

Then, one morning, they are woken by a woman from the ashram office called Sharna. 'Laxmi wants to see you,' she informs K, brightly. 'She asks you to bring your passport.'

While he dresses, Sharna chats to Yamini, who she met in a tantra group months earlier. They are both undergoing hypnotherapy now, and dedicate two hours a day to simply crying. It is clear that Sharna knows nothing, that she is just a messenger.

A rickshaw is waiting downstairs.

Twenty minutes later, all three of them are climbing out of the tiny cabin, at the ashram gates. It is nearly 6am. Yamini squeezes K's hand and rushes off to dynamic meditation. Sharna escorts K to the office. Birds fill the trees above them. The air itself is shining.

Sitting behind her desk, Laxmi is drinking chai. She is expecting him. That same mischievous smile. The same kindness. Her assistant, Sheela, is sitting beside her, talking on the telephone.

'Tell fuck-face I don't give a shit,' Sheela says, clearly enjoying herself.

Laxmi chuckles and gestures to the chair in front of her, inviting K to sit. She is turning an envelope in her hands.

'So,' she says, 'your passport is in order, yes?'

'My passport? Yeah, I think so ...' He hands it over. 'How come?' She flicks through the pages. 'Good.'

His plane ticket will be waiting for him at the airport, she says, passing him the envelope. This is money for the taxi she has booked. Enclosed also is the address of his hotel in Bombay. He has a night in Bombay, and then a flight to Bangkok the following evening. It is simply a precaution, for his own safety. From Bangkok, he is on his own, although it seems that he is expected to make his own way back to Australia. The police are asking questions. The German embassy is involved. Hans had a friend in Poona — not a sannyasin — 'who is wanting to make trouble'.

It takes a moment for this news to land. Hans is dead. K is being sent home.

'It is an accident,' Laxmi assures him. 'It is no one's fault. But there unfortunately won't be time for a leaving darshan.' They will let him know when things have been cleared up. No one is blaming him. Of course he will be welcome to come back when the time is right. Of course. They will let him know. 'Come back soon,' she says, smiling. She has him write down his passport number and his address in Australia.

'Is your father still alive?' she asks.

'My father? Yeah. Why?'

'If anyone asks, he is very sick. This is a good reason to go home, Laxmi thinks, yes?'

These instructions, it is implicit, are coming directly from Bhagwan, and it does not occur to K to question the wisdom of this decision. It is for his own sake, for the good of everyone, for the ashram, but for Bhagwan in particular. Bhagwan must be protected at all costs. His work must continue. It is too important.

He has a headache, but beyond that he doesn't know what he feels. Nothing, perhaps. He thanks Laxmi. Then he stumbles out into the heat of the morning to look for Yamini among the hundred or so people who have already begun dynamic meditation in Buddha Hall.

He pushes through the crowd, searching for her face. Everyone is in orange. They are all breathing hard, their eyes closed, their bodies jolting with the effort of hyperventilation. Finally, he sees her heaving back and forth near the rear of the hall. She is partly obscured by a bamboo post. He gets closer. But maybe it's not Yamini. Maybe it's someone else. She has her eyes closed. But yes, it *is* her. He grabs her by the shoulder, shakes her harder than he means to.

'What's happening?' Her face frightens him. He must look worse than he thinks. He doesn't feel well. He finds himself dragging her back through the crowd.

She pulls her arm away. 'What the fuck's going on?'

Out in the open, he tries to explain the situation: Hans. The German embassy. He is dizzy. Everything feels unreal.

Yamini is looking at him in horror.

'Will you come with me?' he says.

'What? Where?'

'To Melbourne.'

But no. Of course she won't. It's out of the question. And anyway, they hardly know each other.

'I can't,' she says, backing away from him. 'You know I can't. My life is here, with Bhagwan.'

And so it is Abhi who agrees to accompany K back to Bombay. Abhi, who brought him to the ashram in the first place, and who maybe feels some responsibility for what has happened.

'You don't have to come,' K says.

But Abhi is looking forward to it. 'It'll be an adventure,' he says.

Together, back in their ordinary clothes, they take another taxi to Bombay. The whole thing in reverse, but without Mitch and Mark this time.

Prayers bring victory, reads a painted sign on the back window of the taxi, and K hopes it's true, because he has a small wad of pure hash, which he is planning to smuggle back to Australia, up his arse. Mitch — whose name is now Maneesh — had placed it in his hand as they said goodbye. A last-minute parting gift, which he'd accepted blankly, without hope or fear.

'See you when you get back,' Maneesh had said, embracing him. 'I hope everything's okay with your dad.'

K did not know what to say.

In the taxi, too, he does not say much, and even Abhi, after a bout of busy enthusiasm, settles into a silence that is due, in part, to the fear he obviously feels for his own life. The driver keeps his hand on the horn and swerves repeatedly into oncoming traffic. Out the window, a blur of villages and rice paddies and jungle washes away.

It's over, K thinks to himself, though he cannot make the words mean what he wants them to mean. He closes his eyes. He cannot believe what is happening. With every second he is further and further away from Bhagwan.

If death were to come and wipe him out now, a truck or a bus, it wouldn't matter.

—

In Bombay the next morning, Abhi has some business to sort out.

Drugs, K assumes, heroin, but he doesn't ask. He feels as if he is moving in a dream, at half-speed. They arrange to meet in the afternoon.

K spends much of the day staring at the traffic from the hotel window, smoking. There is a vague sense of threat — it is impossible to know how seriously to take it — which is difficult to disentangle from a more general feeling of paranoia. And there is something else, too, lower down in his body and even more frightening: a kind of spreading depression.

The afternoon drags towards evening and still there is no sign of Abhi. Should K be worried? He is. Increasingly, he is desperate with fear and self-pity. He goes downstairs and paces the street, uselessly. He buys cigarettes and a bottle of Campa Cola from a little cart. He gives a relatively large amount of money to a man with no legs. Then he goes back upstairs again and resumes his watch at the window. The day is overcast, oppressive, polluted.

It is almost dark when Abhi finally arrives. He is buoyant as usual. Things have gone well, it seems, it just took much longer than he expected. He apologises, although he doesn't explain. He claps his hands and smiles. He has a secret, that much is clear, but the secret seems, somehow, to include K.

'Lets get something to eat,' he says. 'I'm starving!'

Despite K's intense irritation, Abhi's good mood begins to rub off on him as they sit drinking beer at the Leopold Café. It is strange to be here again, the place where they met. It seems like another life, like a thousand years ago. Abhi orders another round and soon they are wandering through the hot night together, drunk and amazed to be alive on earth, right now, in Bombay. The energy of the city surges through them.

The airport, when they arrive the next evening, is small, makeshift, and surrounded by an aura of intense chaos; an almost impenetrable crowd seethes with travellers and taxi-drivers and beggars and police, with rickshaws, cows, dogs, children. A strange procession winds its way along the footpath and disappears around the corner. There is singing. There are people cooking dinner. There are people lying on the ground, seemingly asleep.

Inside the terminal, it's filthy and unbelievably muggy. The smell of piss and incense is overwhelming. Bent in half, men in white uniforms are carrying huge bags back and forth on their backs. The night outside is like something living, an enormous entity beating at the doors.

'So,' K says. 'This is it. Come visit sometime.' He steps forward to embrace Abhi.

But Abhi pushes him away. 'Not so fast,' he says. 'I'm coming with you.'

'What are you talking about?'

That's what he was doing yesterday, he explains. It wasn't drugs. He was arranging a plane ticket, a visa. 'Amazing what money can do,' he laughs.

Abhi has always wanted to see Australia, he claims. The outback, the dangerous animals.

'I don't know what to say,' K says, genuinely shocked. 'I don't know any dangerous animals.'

And yet, it seems that with this gesture, something has been sealed between them.

Their passage through the various levels of bureaucracy is interminable. Their papers are passed from person to person, checked and re-checked by teams of officials. Someone — it is unclear who — takes their passports and disappears. But fifteen minutes later, the passports are returned with a smile, and eventually they are allowed to board the plane.

For K now, there is a sense, almost, of excitement. A new adventure moving beneath the surface of numb grief. They find their seat numbers, settle in, try to get comfortable. Not exactly easy with a wad of hash up your arse. But it turns out that Abhi has one as well. They laugh about this, in convulsive whispers. They are brothers in arms. Finally, the aeroplane begins to move. It taxies aimlessly around the airport and then, with a tremendous rush, surges forward and lifts into the sky.

Beneath them, India tilts and falls away. Acres of slum shacks pour across the landscape. The black bay is scattered with tankers.

K's hands ache. His arse aches. His head, too. But it will be alright, he thinks. With Abhi, things always turn out alright.

And many hours later, somewhere above Thailand, K reassumes his old name — Vincent. He whispers the word to himself.

Night comes over the cabin.

Beside him, Abhi is asleep. From his ice-speckled window, Vincent looks out and sees, hanging above the earth, a bright moon.

They went all that way just to touch it, he thinks.

PART THREE

Well, we met in Bombay. In Mumbai, I mean. That's what I told him. Or maybe it wasn't Bombay. Maybe it was somewhere else. A café? A hotel lobby? Somewhere there were tables, chairs, windows. Vincent strolled over and said g'day, and pretty quickly I realised I'd found someone who understood. What does that mean? Joe asked. Love, I said. I didn't hesitate to use the word. Or it became a kind of love, anyway. He was a very energetic guy, your dad, that's what I told him, he had a kind of energy about him that appealed to me. Somehow, we just connected. Joe was smiling. He smiled the way Vince used to smile. But sadder. A less energetic smile. He was sitting in that red plastic chair, which he'd dragged in from the front steps. It was weird to see him smile like that. This must have been the first day. Or the second, I suppose. The night of the second. I don't know. The evening. Weeks ago, in other words. But why am I thinking about all this? The same warm breeze through the open window. I was in Mumbai, I said, and your dad came strolling over. And then what happened? he asked. Well, I must have been on my way down to Pune, I told him. I knew a girl who'd got caught up in the meditation scene down there, some sort of experimental ashram, and she used to write me these long letters, really beautiful, totally incomprehensible letters all about her guru and her past lives, and all that sort of stuff. How much she loved me. How much she loved her guru. How much she loved everyone she'd ever met. How she was reliving her former existence as a grey cat. How beautiful it was to hunt and kill, to satisfy her hunger and her instincts. That sort of thing. I had no idea what she was talking about. But she was a very good-looking actress, and my god, she had fantastic breasts. We'd been part of the 'Students for a Democratic Society' together, I think, and actors and actually housemates, for a little while. We'd been in a play together. What was the play? he asked. But I had no idea what the play was. I was smoking a lot of weed in those days, I told him, which was putting it mildly. Anyway, one day she sent me this letter that said: *here I am in India, come find me, I don't know what's going on but everything else is like being half-dead.* The whole world is a zombie apocalypse, basically, that was the general vibe, except for her and all her friends. They were the only human beings left, apparently. Or the only neo-humans. They were an example for the rest of the galaxy, that's what she said. Joe laughed at that, I remember. I don't blame him. And this was the Osho ashram she was talking about? Is that right? Yes, I said, Osho, exactly, isn't that what we're talking about? Although the truth is, I never really liked the name Osho. He was always Bhagwan to me. He still is. Even after he started dressing up like a goddamn Christmas tree, and driving back and forth in Rolls-Royces, and having people follow him round with machine guns. That wasn't the Bhagwan I fell in love with, but he was still Bhagwan, even when he was Osho. Mohan Chandra. Then Acharya Rajneesh. Then Bhagwan

Shree Rajneesh. Then Osho towards the end, after everything had happened, and he needed to rebrand the whole enterprise. You know the story? I asked him. He made some sort of gesture as if to say, yeah, yeah, I know the story, keep talking. So I kept talking. I heard my voice answering his questions, a patient, elderly, frail, faintly cranky voice. Very frail. A whisper really. He had to lean forward to hear what I was saying above the sound of the generator, the sound of the fan, the sound of the singing we could hear coming from across the water when the generator cut out. They were reciting the Bhagavad Gita. This was the first day. Or the second day. One or the other. Back when I could still speak, more or less. I still had a voice then, even if it was the voice of a dying old man. Now, not so much. I can still whisper if I really want to. I can write on a piece of paper. With extraordinary effort I can still roll over and sit up. I can still scratch myself. I can stand. If he takes my weight, it's not too much of a problem to get up and shuffle across to the toilet. My legs tend to buckle without him. The singing has stopped now. How long ago did it stop? Someone is going past in a boat. A warm breeze moves the curtains. A warm breeze strokes the skin of the old man. Which is about as good as it gets. The pleasures of the body, as they say. Memories of other summer evenings. Other open windows and types of paradise. What year would that have been, he asked, when you met Dad? Oh, I don't know, I said. 1976, I guess. Or maybe '77. Basically, I just wanted to find this girl, head up to the Himalayas, walk around, see what was happening. I needed a break from the politics, I told him. The acting. The singing and the dancing. I'd done a stint as a centurion in the stage production of *Jesus Christ Superstar*. We did a lot of street theatre, too. I told him all about it. I heard myself talking and talking. Also, those actions we did: handing out free soup in the park, that sort of thing, wearing a giant goat's head made out of papier-mâché. Also, I was a draft resister. My number didn't come up, but I wrote and told them to go fuck themselves — *I'm not taking part in your racist war*. I don't want to shoot women and babies. I don't want to shoot men, for that matter, either. I don't want to napalm people and burn down their villages, thanks very much. So I was eligible for jail, if they'd wanted to find me, which they probably should have, since I was pretty good friends with some of the people they really *did* want to find. People they did find in the end, and people they didn't. People who went to jail for a long time and others who disappeared for good, like Willy Martin, who went up to Canada and died in great pain, apparently. I never was charged. But the point was to stick your neck out and change the status quo. My father never forgave me for that. He was a war hero. The medals, the nightmares, the whole thing. He was an angry man, a horrible man, really. Trapped in the horror. He flew thirty-three combat missions over Europe in a B-17. In World War Two, you mean? Joe asked. Yes, obviously. I admired him immensely for that. And then the Vietnam War happened, and everything changed. I grew my hair. I went to all the protests. I was there when Abbie Hoffman made the Pentagon levitate. I met Abbie. I wouldn't say we were friends. But we knew about each other. We knew other people who knew each other. My father was very unforgiving. He was deeply offended. He took it as a personal insult. I was dead to him for a long time. But the last thing in the world I wanted was to end up like him, a broken, really deeply broken, very wealthy man, screaming in his sleep. Which, incidentally, is not far from what's happened, despite my best intentions. I have the nightmares, anyway. Not the money. My father disinherited me. After he died at the end of

'87, I went up to see his lawyer. Turned out he'd given all his money to a right-wing think-tank called Center for the American Future —— real nice people. It was a surprise, but not that much of a surprise. I still dream about my father. Horrible dreams, especially since I got here. A lifetime of built-up psychic detritus, unspooling in the head. Some sort of clean-out before I'm evicted for good. Dreams, memories, nightmares. Call them whatever you want, I said. Or maybe I didn't say all of this. Maybe I just thought it. Dreams about my mother, too. But mostly my father. What did your father do? he asked at some point, so I must have been telling him about my father. He was an engineer, I said. He worked for Boeing after the war. That was another thing I was very proud about, the little component he helped design for the Saturn V rocket. Some sort of little gizmo thing they used for steering the outer engines. I loved the moon landing. The whole Apollo thing. Armstrong's dignity. My father's crucial role. The future of human endeavour. I was obsessed for a long time. I was less proud, as I got older, of my father's contribution to the design of military helicopters. Then he left Boeing and went into commercial plastic bags. That was the future. First space travel, then war, then plastic bread-bags, in that order. You'd think maybe they got the order wrong, but no. That's human progress for you. Then Mobil bought him out, and he became a big millionaire and retired, and began drinking seriously. Did he ever talk about the war? Joe asked. No, I said. No. He never did. Not to me, certainly. So it's impossible to say how many people he was responsible for killing, or, to put it differently, how many of them were Nazis. But one of my earliest memories is the sound of my father screaming in his sleep. The sound of my mother saying his name. I remember that. Also, the way he'd put you up against the wall, sometimes. Me, I mean. With his elbow in your throat. And now every time I see a plastic bag floating in the wind or clogging up a river, it's like coming face-to-face with him again. With his mighty and more or less endless contribution to the world. But I was telling Joe how I'd arrived in India. That's what we were talking about. I was twenty-three years old, and I was burnt out by all the protests, the actions, the acting, the readily available and not particularly expensive drugs. I slept in a lot of different places. Streets, hills, cars, barns, treehouses, rooms that belonged to people I'd never met. But I don't think I slept very much. Under bridges. I was very tired. We were all exhausted for some reason. I don't know why we were so tired. We were children. We were burning up. Anyway, the war was finished. A lot of people were going mad. People I knew. What was going to happen now? An old friend jumped off the Golden Gate Bridge. His name escapes me. But we were pretty good buddies. Another guy I knew OD'd. There were lots of guys like that. It was a strange time. I wanted a different kind of adventure. The day Patty Hearst got sentenced, I was on an aeroplane. So that was, what, 1976, I guess. I flew to Turkey and somehow I got talking to this English couple, real drug-addled hippies, and we ended up driving their Land Rover down through Syria and Iran, and up into the north of Afghanistan. We woke up in a field one morning surrounded by Afghan warlords. Amazing people. Amazing orchards. Amazing lakes. After that we travelled down to India, and then we split up and went our different ways. He died of pneumonia, I think, later on. Who did? Joe said. The English guy. I've forgotten his name. I don't know what happened to her. Susie, I think her name was. Susie. We lost touch. But we had a good time. Those were the days when Charles Sobhraj was going around murdering backpackers and stealing their passports. I was in India during the state of emergency. They were stoning the trains, they were trying to shoot Indira Gandhi. It was a fantastic time to be alive. It was chaos. And then at some point, I guess, I must have been in Bombay, in Mumbai, and Vincent came strolling over. And what was he like? Joe asked. Well, he had a kind of swagger to him in those days, I said, and it's true. He did. He had a kind of tough-guy thing, with the tatts and everything, which of course he wasn't. Or maybe he was. But if that's the case it was before my time, so how would I know? But he liked to put it on a bit, I think. He liked people to think he was a tough guy. He had a boldness about him, which I liked straight away. He was a funny guy. I don't remember what we talked about, but I remember Vincent being very, very sad and lonely because he'd just split up with some girl back home. Someone called Astra? Joe said. Was that her name? Do you remember? But I didn't. I don't. Maybe, I said. Could have been Astra. Anyway, we decided to get drunk on whatever we could find. We found some horrible, really horrible, horrible red wine, just undrinkable, and we drank that and some other things. Maybe we found ourselves some Indian whiskey too. Probably not. It wasn't easy finding alcohol in Mumbai in those days, but it wasn't impossible. He was a big drinker, your dad, I told him. A big smoker, too. He smoked a lot of weed. We all did. A lot of hash, which in India, in those days, was really gorgeous stuff. Anyway, we'd just met each other so, true to form, we decided to celebrate. I still had about three hundred and fifty *Jesus Christ Superstar* dollars in my pocket, maybe even more, which was a hell of a lot of money in India in those days, and I knew if things ever got desperate, I could always go home and kiss my dad's arse for a while, and there'd probably be another million and a half waiting for me when he died, provided I kissed hard enough. I would have had to kiss pretty goddamn hard. But still. Not impossible. Not that I was planning on doing it. I'd made my break from him already. A semi-break, let's call it. I'd gone to India. I wasn't planning on coming back any time soon. I'd told my father, maybe with less conviction than I should have, where he could stick his ransom money. I didn't say ransom. What I'm saying is, I've never felt money to be an issue, even when I was standing out the front of some church or another waiting for a free peanut-butter sandwich. It comes and goes. I've never clung to it. So we went to a fancy restaurant, Vince and I. A really confusing place with too many waiters or too many mirrors or both. But the food was excellent. I love Indian food. South Indian. North Indian. All of it. I used to anyway. It's hard to eat now. Hard to swallow. Just a little bit of this and that. A little bit of coconut rice, some stewy things served on a banana leaf. There's a nice Indian family next door who cook for me. Anitha and Kumeran. Lovely people. Maybe that's what they're doing right now. Organising something next door. Some idiyappam. Some appam with ishtu. Some beer and whiskey, too. I hope so. Although they're Catholics and they don't approve of alcohol. But I don't remember what Vince and I ate in Bombay forty-five bloody years ago, if that's what you're asking. I remember we talked about the organisations we'd belonged to back home, that sort of thing, and the actions we'd undertaken in the name of the revolution. Vince had been into all of that back in Melbourne too, or so he claimed. You probably know more about this than I do, I told Joe, but he shook his head. No, he said. He didn't know much about it. His dad had never told him much about anything. Or maybe he had, but he hadn't been listening, which is probably more likely. Anyway, we found ourselves at the ashram, eventually, I told him. We took a taxi or maybe it was a train, I don't remember. This is all a long time ago, so maybe none of this is true. I loved the trains. The trains were like wombs, you just lay there and everything you needed came to your window, it was fantastic. I guess they're still like that. Rocky fields beside the train tracks, growing nothing. And then the landscape would change, and you'd be in the bloody jungle all of a sudden, the sun through the trees, the villages, the goats, the little cups of tea, the little treats. Kids running beside the train tracks, trying to keep up. It was a beautiful time. I was blessed. I really was. It was a golden age. And I vowed never to come back and ruin it. Why risk your fondest memories? I certainly never wanted to go back to Pune, that's for sure, to the ashram. I'll never do that. I've got a pretty good idea of what they've done to the place, because they send me emails, and I still haven't figured out how to unsubscribe from their bloody mailing list. All that fascist, corporate mysticism really gives me the shits. It looks like an airport now. But here I am in India, anyway. I did come back. I couldn't help myself. The idea was always there, nagging away. India gets into you, doesn't it? Maybe, he said. I don't really know yet. Well, there you go, each to their own. But in any case, I got an email out of the blue one day from an old ashram buddy called Maneesh, I told him. Formally Mitch Marlett. Canadian guy I hadn't heard of since the Oregon days, the early eighties. He found my address somehow, and sent me a long, heartfelt letter from the jail cell where he was serving the last five months of a three-year sentence for gem smuggling. This was years ago now. He must have seen that episode of *Law and Order* I did, I think that was the only show they were allowed to watch in there, poor buggers, but every year since he got out, Maneesh invited me down to Kerala for a full-moon party. He had a place I could stay, he kept telling me, which he was looking after for somebody else. Paradise, he kept saying. Not that I care about full-moon parties. I don't know why I accepted. Or maybe I do. I guess I do. Paradise sounds nice, doesn't it. But also, things had started to change at home. The body had started to go. The body is a temple and the temple had started to fall apart, as temples do eventually. I'd begun to trip over. Nothing exceptional. I'd started to lose strength in my legs, in my hands. *This is it*, I thought. *It's coming for you.* Did I really want to die alone in a tiny little flat on the outskirts of Sydney? No, I did not. With carpet like that? Wandering through the supermarket sometimes, my legs would stutter. Suddenly, someone would be picking me up off the ground. Some pretty young thing. I'd be lying on the ground staring up at the fluorescent lights. Blinded. *So here it is*, I'd think. Most days I didn't believe it. But then I started to. Now I do, obviously. Now there's no denying anything. Now I hobble around with a walking stick and struggle to swallow, which means I can't ignore what I've been hoping to ignore for a while longer — namely death, namely Lou Gehrig's disease, which is what killed my father, and which also killed my father's brother and sister, and their father too, probably. It's a disease I've anticipated for a long time, because the chances of my having it have always been fifty-fifty. It's been riding towards me for generations, like a wave that's finally breaking over the top of my head. So I told Maneesh, okay, I'm coming. I caught a plane. I arrived in India again. It was two in the morning. I did what everyone else did and put my bag through the X-ray machine, even though there was nobody there to operate it. Then I walked out into the night. India again. The decades come pouring back. It's true. I was frightened, but I was happy, even if things had changed a bit in the last forty years. I caught a taxi. It was like coming home. I caught a train through the jungle. I lay on my little bunk and witnessed an endless procession of beggars and touts and blind sadhus and lepers with no fingers and women sweeping on their hands and knees. This is what I remembered. But why so fondly? I got out and caught another taxi, and all the happiness rushed in through the open windows. The Arabian Sea out there, the green ponds stranded on the beach. Palm trees. All the stuff you dream about when someone says paradise too often. I hardly recognised Maneesh when I saw him, he was so fat. He was topless. He was wearing one of those Indian skirts, like a sadhu. He was running a joint on the beach called the Café le Space. He called himself a DJ. He looked ridiculous. But no more ridiculous than me, probably. He'd just had a whole new set of teeth inserted into his gums, in Mumbai. Very affordably. That's something I won't have to look forward to. We found another taxi. We came out here. This is more or less what I told Joe, I think. And so here I am now, lying in this little brick building, not much more than a room really, hidden among palm trees, a long, long way from all the tourists, about fifteen metres from the water. The warm breeze strokes my skin. And if someone helps me, I can still walk down to the water. Paradise, Maneesh kept saying, although it's more rudimentary than paradise, in my opinion. Still, the rent is hardly anything. The place belongs to a man who'll be in jail for another year and a half at least, which is more than enough time. I'll be gone before then. But there's something else as well. Because if it wasn't for Joe calling me up out of the blue and sounding so much like Vincent, I doubt I would have had the inclination to fling myself back into the past like this. I doubt I'd have had the courage or the stupidity, for that matter, since, in my condition, the past holds endlessly more than the future and for that reason, doing anything to jeopardise the past is really just a disaster waiting to happen. Which might be exactly what this is. But is it his disaster or mine? I wondered, looking at Joe sitting there in that red plastic chair. What happened when you got to the ashram? he asked. Was Dad there? That's what we were talking about. Vince. Of course he was there, I told him, we walked in together. And the truth is, I remember that part very clearly. I'll never forget it. We walked through the gates, and I just felt this warm fuzzy feeling. Like I really was coming home. It was like being in your mother's arms again, I said. Well maybe not *my* mother's arms, but you know what I mean. And there were all these beautiful people walking around, beautiful women and beautiful men, probably a couple hundred of them, dancing together and going crazy and wearing orange and wearing beads. It blew my mind. And then we met Laxmi, who was Bhagwan's secretary at the time, a really lovely person, and she said: Are you ready for sannyas? And we said we didn't know. What do you reckon? And she said, okay good, well you come tonight, have a shower, get yourself some orange clothes, don't smoke any cigarettes before you come, lay off the weed. Don't get all fucked up on anything. So we rocked up that night or whenever it was, it could have been the night after that, and we sat down, and they called our names out, I think I was the first to be called, and I went up and sat in front of Bhagwan's feet and he told me to close my eyes, and then after a while he said, you can open your eyes now, and he put the mala over my head, and he started telling me what my new name was going to mean, Abhiyāna, which means divine adventure. And what was Osho like? Joe asked. Bhagwan, you mean? Yeah Bhagwan, he said. He was funny as fuck, I said. He was extraordinary. And that's the truth. He was this just tiny, immaculate kind of guy, very graceful, but also

somehow enormous, like a mountain. It's hard to explain. He was an
outrageous old bastard. And he had this look on his face, like the whole
thing was a big joke. Life, I mean. All these people, taking themselves
so seriously. And what I thought was: *here is my true father.* Or I felt it,
I guess. I don't think I thought anything. It was like a silent explosion.
Or an implosion. Like something just falling away. It was really just the
feeling of being home, at last, you know. *You can stop searching. You can
relax. Everything is going to be fine. There's absolutely nothing to worry
about. All there is, is Love. Simple as that.* But when he looked into my
eyes, I saw there was nobody there. Where was he? Joe asked. I've got
no idea, I said. He was just an empty vessel. He was a complete and
utter fucking loony-tune. The whole thing was like a dream. Like a
what? Joe said. He couldn't hear me. My voice was very frail then. It's
basically gone now, but it was very frail then. The muscles in my throat
are dying. Like a dream, I yelled. Oh right, a dream, he said. Okay.
Cool, go on. What happened next? What did Bhagwan say? I don't
know, I told him. Suddenly, I didn't feel like going on. I can't remember,
I said. You don't remember any of what he said? he asked. Not a thing,
I said. But it's true, I felt totally penetrated. Penetrated? he said. Yes, I
said, penetrated. Bhagwan was channelling something. It was like the
universe was just pouring through him. And if you didn't experience it,
then you won't understand. It was like every cell in my body was
vibrating. I had to be carried away. What? Joe said, leaning towards
me. He couldn't understand a word I was saying. The great orator's
voice was gone. It was like the last few drops of juice from a straw,
dribbling out. The whole thing had been sucked dry. Not that I ever got
the chance to be the great orator I could have been. I played the Duke
of Albany once in a very average production of *Lear* we did up at The

Mount, in Massachusetts. But the Duke of Albany is not much of an orator. I was a great B-grade movie criminal instead, a great victim of straight-to-video B-grade violence. I was thrown through windows, shot, stabbed, kicked, dumped out in the desert to die. My body was eaten by coyotes. I rose again to become a great voice-over actor in an ad for Colgate toothpaste in 1987. I was a fairly decent drug-baron in *Time to Die* in 1992 with Lorenzo Lamas, and a passable corrupt lawyer in an episode of *Law and Order*. I was a half-hearted ageing alien bounty-hunter in series 2 of *Shadow Worlds*, which never went to air. That was a terrible production. We all knew it was terrible. Morale was very low. And now the voice is gone completely. And what did Bhagwan say to Dad? Joe asked. He had a look in his eyes now, Joe, like he was closing in on me, I thought. He was staring at me. He looked like he hadn't slept properly for weeks. He brushed at the air. The beautiful green bodies of flies buzzed around us. They are still buzzing now, all these weeks later, or months, as the case may be, like miraculous jewels that die and get reborn almost instantly. And what did Bhagwan say? he asked again. How would I know? I said. And that's true, I couldn't remember anything that happened after he put the mala over my head. I had to be carried back to my seat, I told him. I was totally fucked. I wasn't listening to anything anyone was saying. I'd been changed into someone else. Joe nodded as if he understood, but it was clear he didn't really understand. He didn't, and he couldn't. How could he? He wasn't there. And nothing I could say meant anything. They were just words, signs, when the true thing is sign-less. You'd be fucking crazy to believe any of this, I told him. But what happened to Dad, he asked. Did Dad join up? Of course he joined up, I said. That's what taking sannyas means. It means you've joined up.

You're in the gang. You mean the cult, he said. Well, sure, if you want to get technical, I said. And I think he laughed then, we both laughed, but not in a happy way. And what was Dad like after that? he asked. What do you mean? I said. I mean, was he changed? After he took sannyas? Did something happen to him? I looked him in the eyes. He was sitting beside the bed. Light was falling into the room through the window. Late afternoon light. Then the light faded, and the room became dark again. He really didn't look good. He was a middle-aged man now. Tired, sunburnt. His eyes were bloodshot. The skin was peeling off his face. He reeked of despair. Here is a man, I thought, who reeks of despair, and who desperately wants what I have to give. But would I give it to him? He'd come all this way just to hear it. And where was his family? He had a wife and a kid. He'd told me that much. He'd left them behind to come out here and talk to me. He'd told me he was here for a conference, but I knew he was lying about that. A conference? I'd said. Oh yeah, what sort of conference? Oh, nothing interesting, he said, just university stuff. Cross-cultural relationship building, that sort of thing. Just marketing, he said. But he was not a good actor. On the other side of the river they were still singing, chanting. They've stopped now. But back then they were still chanting. I miss that. The Bhagavad Gita. We could hear bells and water birds, and the sound of kids chucking a plastic Coca-Cola bottle back and forth in the shallow water, like they do most days at about that time, although I didn't hear them today. I don't think I did. I can't remember. How was Dad different after he met Bhagwan? Joe asked. Your dad was crazy, I told him. He was even crazier than ever. But no crazier than the rest of us, no crazier than I was, that's for sure. We were all crazy. *Just be total*, that's what the saying was. That was the whole point. Normality is insanity, or maybe that was a different saying. We were crazy with love. We really were. We were superhumans, mutants. We were blessed. Every day felt like a week. We laughed and laughed. We laughed a lot. I know we cried a lot, too. Particularly the men. The men cried, I told him; the women, not so much. The women punched you in the face and chucked your shit out the window and abused you. The women were tough as nails. They had foul mouths. The men sat around crying and talking about their feelings. The women turned into men and the men turned into women. Really? Joe said, sounding unconvinced. But that was the truth. Or it felt like the truth. And at the end of the day, we all did a lot of fucking. A lot, a lot. There were absolutely no noes. Maybe there should have been, but there weren't. I was there for four years in Pune and another two and a half in Oregon. Six years of my life. But it feels like sixty. Like a whole lifetime. I've lived twice, I told him, once with Bhagwan and once everywhere else, and I know which one I preferred, that's for sure. Joe looked at me then, and I saw Vincent's face suddenly looking at me. I remember this very clearly. I can see it now. Vincent's beautiful smile. It was uncanny. He was smiling, encouraging me to go on. And I was happy to see him, Joe, I mean, and not only because I knew that the time was coming when I would need his help. When I would need him to help me roll over in bed and get up and go to the toilet. I would need him to adjust my respirator and get me to the hospital along dirt roads and back again. All the things that he does now, in other words. Shopping. Riding out to the shops to collect my medicine. Cleaning up. Sweeping spiders from the dusty floor. The work of a loyal son. Not that I plan on lingering. I do not. I do not plan on having a colostomy bag or a feeding tube. I draw the line there. I see myself taking my last sip of

Nembutal while I can still swallow, sitting down there by the water, listening to those kids chucking that plastic Coke bottle back and forth. And that day is not far away. But something happened, didn't it? Joe said, leaning towards me again. His face was very close. I could smell him. I'm sure he could smell me too. We were both sweating, but I remember he was sweating a *lot*. It was rolling off him. You and Dad came back to Melbourne together, he said, and something hard had come into his voice. What happened? Why did he leave the ashram? Why did he never tell me about it? The room was filling up with mosquitoes. Little evil ones. We had arrived at the crux of the problem, if that's what you want to call it. The fork in the road. The little engine that was driving the whole thing. It was late afternoon. The grey sky was boiling. A luminous torpor prevailed. The air was damp. And suddenly, for no reason I can think of, or maybe it was because of the weather, the strange heat or the strange look in Joe's eyes, I had a memory of the Ranch in Oregon, of Rajneeshpuram, the City of the Lord of the Full Moon, and of leaving the ranch one morning and riding a motorbike up to Seattle, to visit my father for his sixty-fifth birthday. Suddenly, I started telling him this story. I'd got special permission to leave, which hardly ever happened in those days, even if it was an emergency. Often they didn't let you leave. I mean, you could always leave, but maybe you couldn't come back again. Anyway, for some reason they said fine, take three weeks off. Have a holiday, you don't look so good. I don't know why. And Sheela, you know who Sheela was? I asked him. Yeah, Joe said, I know who she was. Well, by this stage, Sheela had replaced Laxmi as Bhagwan's secretary. It wasn't the same old ashram. I never got along with Sheela. She never liked me, and I never liked her. It was a mystery to me how Bhagwan could stand to be in the same room with her, to be honest. Anyway, things were different by that stage, that's what I was trying to say. In what way were they different? Joe asked. Well, to start with, it was a ranch, not an ashram. To start with, we were in the middle of bloody Oregon instead of India. And by this point, of course, Bhagwan was no longer giving discourse. He'd gone into silence. I missed him. I missed him a lot. I still do, the old bugger. Plus, there was all sorts of legal bullshit going on which was not, and still isn't, very interesting. Bullshit like machine guns? Joe said. Well, there was that too, I said. But I'm talking about bullshit to do with zoning laws and elections. And what about how they poisoned the salad bars? Joe said. Yeah, yeah, sure, I said, but we didn't know about any of that stuff. All that stuff was a big secret. That was just a few fucking crazy people at the top. Everything else was fantastic, most of the time I mean. Most of the time it was just a really beautiful, harmonious, sophisticated, creative, loving kind of place. It was a family. It was a farm, it was a commune, it was a kind of labour camp for a while there, but it wasn't a mystery school anymore, I guess that's what I was trying to say. It wasn't like Pune. Anyway, I was working in construction at this point, driving a great big bulldozer round and round. I was doing twelve-hour days, seven days a week in a giant, muddy paddock. I was exhausted. I was probably sick. I'd recovered from hepatitis. I'd recovered from a lot of different things. I know I was depressed, although I don't think I knew it at the time. Maybe that's why they let me go. Too much negative energy. I hardly saw Bhagwan anymore, except when he drove past every day at two o'clock in the afternoon in a Rolls Royce and waved. But mostly I didn't bother with that. I hadn't gone all that way just to watch someone drive around in his car. It was my father's birthday, and for some reason they let me go.

I borrowed this guy's motorcycle, a great big Russian Cossack motorcycle, and I rode three hundred miles up to Seattle. It was fantastic. It took me a week to get there. One night I slept in the woods outside some little bum-shit town I can't remember the name of. I fished in a river and caught a whopping big trout that I cooked on the fire and ate, and I thought *this is the fucking life*, but then I started to get really paranoid. I must have been smoking something pretty heavy, because I had the feeling that rednecks were going to come and murder me in my sleep, just like they murdered Jack Nicholson, if you know what I mean. Before that I stayed a few nights in Portland with a friend of mine, an old ashram friend from Pune. Her name was Yamini, which meant Nighttime or Starry Night or Peaceful Night or Night of Ashes or something like that. We'd been in love in Pune, and she'd already left the ranch by this stage. I guess, we were somehow soulmates. I stayed with her for a couple days. On the last night she asked me to move in with her. I said I'd think about it. I still think about it, if you want to know the truth. She had a job as a waitress in a burger place, but she'd worked in the publishing department in Pune, and she was hoping to get a job as an editorial assistant for an academic publisher. She was really lonely, because she'd been kicked off the ranch and she wasn't allowed to go back again. She'd had a falling out with Sheela, and now no one would talk to her. None of her friends. She was blacklisted. I mean, it was a big thing that I was there. She thought her phone was bugged. It could have been, for all I know. She thought people were following her. I remember her house was really dark, and she kept looking out the window. She had a housemate, this Scottish guy, who only ate brown rice, basically. But I didn't meet him until the second night. The first night, Yamini and I stayed up drinking and talking and doing everything else, and then on the second night, her housemate came home, and we all got pretty high and then at some point he locked himself in the bathroom and refused to come out. He was in love with Yamini, I think. On the third night, Yamini told me she wanted me to stay. She wanted to get married. Her visa was about to expire. She was English. Half English, half Italian. She couldn't have children, but we could adopt, she said. I told her I didn't know if I could do any of that. I wasn't ready for it. I wasn't ready to leave Bhagwan. In the morning we had a disastrous breakfast together. I remember she hardly spoke, and she didn't eat anything, although I ate a lot — for some reason I was incredibly hungry. And then I left and went to a couple other places, and two or three days later I rode up to my father's house in Broadmoor, which is a posh part of Seattle. It was late in the afternoon when I arrived. My father had this big two-storey mansion. I'd never been there before, but my brother had given me the address. I don't know what I was expecting. It was an overcast day, really super-muggy, and there were people in cocktail dresses and dinner jackets standing around sweating on the lawn and drinking little drinks. I saw my brother. I saw my father's new girlfriend. I saw my father. I was wearing an orange jumpsuit. It was 1983. My father saw me, and he walked across the lawn with two glasses in his hand, two glasses of single malt bloody whatever. I thought he looked pretty good for a sixty-five-year-old war veteran — he was tanned and healthy — although three years later he'd be dead. I remember I went up to him and said, happy birthday you old bugger, something like that, and I put my arms out. I hadn't seen him for years, it was a surprise, I hadn't told him I was coming, and he looked at me and said: What is this? I don't recognise you, I want you off of my goddamn fucking property dressed like that. So that was the end of it. It wasn't the last time I saw him, but it was probably the last time I saw him walking around. This was what I was thinking about or what I was telling Joe. I don't know why. He hadn't said anything for a long time. But I remember I was suddenly very, very tired. Breathing was tiring. Eating and drinking were tiring. But talking was supernaturally tiring. Not to mention remembering. It was almost dark by this point. We could hear dogs. We heard something splashing in the water nearby. At some point, Joe stood up and went to the door, as if he expected someone to be there. I felt a gentle breeze, almost cool. Dead spiders, light as cotton, drifted across the floor. Joe turned back to me. Are there monkeys out here? he asked. No, I said, I don't think monkeys come this far south. He nodded. Okay, he said, and then what happened? What happened when? I asked. At the party, he said. Oh, well, then I got back on my motorbike and rode away, I said. My mother was in a nursing home nearby, but she had dementia, and I knew she wouldn't recognise me either. She'd been there for years; she didn't know who I was. So I didn't visit her. I thought about it, but I decided not to. Did you go back and see Yamini? he asked. No, I said. I rode straight back to the ranch. That was my family. Joe was looking at me. He looked sick, I thought. Like something was wrong with him or like he was very hungover. He came back and sat down beside the bed again. What does it feel like? he asked eventually. What does *what* feel like? I said. Lou Gehrig's disease, he said. Well, it's not that nice, I told him. It's like being slowly paralysed. Your legs, your hands, your throat. It gets hard to swallow. It's not very easy to drink this beer, for instance, as you might have noticed. So maybe there's worse ways to go, but I don't know many of them. He nodded and sat back in his chair. It was dark by that time. Light the lamp, I told him.

There are matches over there on the shelf. Okay, he said. It took him a while, but he figured it out. The singing had stopped for the night. We listened to the sound of the gas lamp. The insects. We were drinking warm beer. I remember a very long silence. And what about Dad? he asked at last. You didn't answer the question. Why did he leave the ashram? What happened? Nothing happened as far as I know, I told him. Your grandfather was sick, I said. Vince went home to see him. That's what happened. But my grandfather lived until he was ninety years old, he said, he was basically invincible, he was like a bull that couldn't die. I shrugged. So what was wrong with him, then? Joe asked. No idea, I said. I can't remember. I guess it was a false alarm. And from there the rest was easy enough. I'd made up my mind. We'd made up our minds a long time ago, hadn't we? That was the agreement. You were my brother, and that's what you wanted. So I knew the script pretty well. I half-believed it anyway, after all those years. I said my lines. I wasn't bad. Your dad went home and met your mum and settled down, I told him. Your mum got pregnant. You were born. Life happened, I said. That's what happened. Which was more or less the truth anyway, wasn't it? After you were born, I told him, your dad couldn't do that sort of shit anymore. Hanging out with crazy hippies. He put it all behind him. And maybe I half-wondered who I was trying to protect. You? Bhagwan? The past in general? But it didn't really matter anymore. You were both gone. All that stuff was finished now. It was just smoke in the head. By that point, anyway, the whole thing had started to annoy me. All the questions and answers. I was exhausted. And what happened to Yamini? Joe asked. She's dead, I told him. She died. When did she die? he asked. A long time ago.

PART FOUR

The phone rang and rang.

'Yeah?' a man finally said.

It might have been her dad, but there was no video, and she'd barely spoken to her dad in the last couple of years, so it might not have been him. He didn't believe in normal phones. Also, he'd installed some thing so the government couldn't monitor him, and which made his voice sound weird. Sylvie thought about hanging up.

'Dad?' she said.

Immediately, his voice softened.

She told him she'd be driving down to see her mum in Melbourne. Maybe she could come past on the way through? Not that it wasn't out of the way. It was. It was a long way out of the way, in the bush somewhere, or the desert, or whatever.

'Of course, mate,' he said. 'No worries.'

He didn't ask why she wanted to come. Which was good, because she couldn't have told him.

'Anyway, I'll come out the day after tomorrow,' she said.

'Thursday, if you're going to be there.' Blankly, she turned her mind from the implications of this statement.

She could always cancel.

Her dad was saying something to someone else that she couldn't understand. There was a woman's voice in the background. Short, harsh sentences. Then he said: 'Just happens I got a fresh vacancy. Number seven.'

'You mean someone died?'

There was a pause. 'I'll fix her up for you, Vee. You can stay as long as you want. You know that.'

It wasn't much of an offer — she knew *that*.

'But you'll call me again if you really are coming?' he said.

'I'm coming on Thursday,' she told him. 'Really. I just said that. I'm calling you now.'

That was the plan, anyway, but by Thursday afternoon, Sylvie realised she couldn't do it. She was still three hours away, and the map said there was a place called Esperance up ahead, which was still going. She clicked on it. It had a service station and a motel. She clicked on the motel, skipped through a short promotional video. The place looked okay. Or not nightmarish, anyway, and the reviews weren't terrible. She zoomed out again. There was an Italian restaurant in the main street — La Strada Affamata — and a pub with no obvious fascist paraphernalia. She took the car off autopilot, unzipped the Vista — a view of lush Asian jungle — and pulled onto the exit, which was lined on either side, she saw now, by long rows of blackened trunks, from which luminous green foliage had begun to sprout. A fire had come through not so long ago, but Esperance had survived, apparently. So she would sleep in Esperance and give herself another night to think about it. Maybe she'd feel stronger in the morning. Or maybe she wouldn't. Maybe she'd drive straight through and forget all about it. Two years, three years. What difference would it make?

But when she got to Esperance, she saw that the map was wrong. The whole town had been abandoned. The streets were empty. There was graffiti smeared across everything.

She pulled over and parked beneath a flaking sign that said *Esperance Sands Motel* and got out of the car.

Dull heat. The loneliness of wind across sandy fields. No birds, just flecks of black plastic, and higher up, she guessed, the sturdier bodies of tiny drones.

She walked across the road, not knowing what she was looking for, then through the motel carpark and out under a brown-brick archway that led to the rear of the building. Far-off dogs barked. Rubbish skittered past.

Standing beside the empty swimming pool, she spoke to her watch. She'd been offline almost twelve hours. Much more than that would raise alarms. The screen shimmered open, and she approved connect. One hundred and eighty-five messages. Fifty-seven fresh videos. Thirty-one calls. Harlow. Frida. Her mum. The office. Both bar jobs. The government loans office. Her SkinSuit required updating. Her credit rating had dropped three points. Also, new emergency procedures, and a bunch of automated government messages requesting her to verify her identity, because she'd been offline for more than eight hours. The accumulated messages disgorged their tiny vibrations through her. Twelve hours' worth. A rush. She sifted for Harlow.

Seventeen fresh videos.

She chose the most recent. Nine minutes ago.

He appeared to be sitting on the edge of a skyscraper, strumming a dumb tune on his guitar. His legs dangling in fluffy clouds.

'Oh baby, you're still offline,' he sang. 'I want you to come back and be mine oh mine.'

In the distance, Mount Fuji or something was disgorging rainbow coloured love-hearts.

'I promise, babe, I'll be better this time,' he sang. 'Everything is gonna be fi-i-ine!'

She considered calling him, but a door was banging repetitively behind her in the wind. Turning, she caught sight of her own reflection in the window, and was briefly annoyed at her hair, and then at herself for caring about it. She decided not to call. She dropped offline, felt the sad offline tune play through her. That plunging feeling, like a kind of grief. It mingled with the nausea in a way that seemed about right. She'd been chewing apple-flavoured gum, but apple flavour no longer did the trick. Ginger was what she needed, but she was all out of ginger. Also, she had a painful ulcer in her mouth. Also, she was pregnant. The reality lurched through her again. No one she knew had ever been pregnant. She was thirty-one years old, and she didn't want a baby. Obviously. She and Harlow had agreed about that a long time ago, though neither of them had got round to having the op. The op was insanely expensive. As would be what she'd have to do now. She wasn't sure how they were going to afford it, which was, of course, the idea. But it was cruel to bring a child into the world. Cruel and selfish. That was still Harlow's position. '*Our* position,' he had clarified, and she had hated him for that, though he had meant, or had meant to mean — and she knew this — not simply his and her position, but rather *The Group*'s position, the whole reason they lived where they lived, the precondition for their apparent semi-happiness. If that was indeed what it was. It was a communal set-up across seven houses in suburban Sydney. They had goats and bees and grew a lot of their own food, though Sylvie wasn't particularly interested in that aspect of the arrangement. She liked the parties, the big dinners, the easy way you could come and go in a crowd. She liked standing on the roof at dusk, high on whatever, in music, watching the bats come over. There were twenty-five adults and no kids. That was the position.

'*Our* position?' she'd replied, seeing herself outraged as if from afar, but not quite believing it.

Harlow had come towards her. 'What I meant,' he'd said. 'Babe, come on. You know what I mean. Don't be like that.'

That was three days ago. They had been standing in the kitchen, with the smell of burning goat's milk. Frida had walked in, winced at Sylvie, and left. Frida knew what was happening. Sylvie had told them already, because Frida and Sylvie still had a thing together, too. Harlow smiled exaggeratedly. He had a funny, privileged kind of intelligence, a restless energy she had found infuriating and lovely when they first met. She still found it that. His mind skipped along like a puppy with all that theoretical Marxist bravado. Then he would suddenly slip into profound depression and be gone from her for days. He'd reached out and tried to touch her face.

'Babe, don't pretend to misunderstand me,' he said.

She stepped back. 'I understand you, mate. Don't you worry.'

So here she was. Alone for the first time in what felt like ages. Pregnant, in a derelict motel in the middle of nowhere. Strangely, she didn't feel depressed. Tired, but not depressed. Maybe even kind of alive. The day before yesterday felt like a long time ago, as if weeks had been drained from her.

She watched a dog trot across the carpark and disappear behind a low wall. Then another dog, smaller than the first, with a faint limp. Since leaving Sydney, her vision had become more acute. Edging out of the city, hours earlier, passing through the endless checkpoints and mounds of uncollected garbage, she had felt thrillingly awakened to such seemingly insignificant moments: a shirtless man dancing in his apartment, three dirty feet protruding from the doorway of a tent on the footpath, an enormous piece of wet lettuce rising slowly into the air above the traffic lights, while a booming voice declared, *Never Less than Fresh*. Sylvie had imagined an enormous man strapped to a chair, a giant, forced to repeat this phrase indefinitely. And then a little girl had come begging towards her through the stalled traffic. A nine- or ten-year-old girl with the expression of a thirty-year-old woman, haughty and determined, hefting her baby brother on her hip as she moved from car to car, beneath the lettuce.

The door behind her kept banging. A dog barked again, closer this time. The day had suddenly become cold. Sylvie's legs were cold. The sun had gone down behind the motel. She shouldn't hang around. Scavengers prowled places like this. Teams of dusty men. She walked back through the carpark. On the other side of the road, above the grey fields, the sky looked like an old painting: unreal white clouds at even distances. Flat, pleasant blue between them.

The car sat gleaming where she'd left it on the gravel, and she was suddenly grateful for its loyalty, though of course it wasn't hers. It belonged to Harlow's mother, Ana, but Ana was away, and Sylvie hadn't asked to borrow it because she wasn't talking to Harlow. So technically, she supposed, it was stolen. Ana worked in Hong Kong now — she managed an art fund that was indirectly owned by the same Chinese company that was mining the moon — but she and Sylvie got along when they occasionally saw each other, much to Harlow's annoyance. They shared an interest in old paintings. Sylvie had only driven this car once before, years earlier, with Harlow, when it was brand new.

'It should be illegal to own a car worth this much,' Harlow had said.

But there they were, driving it anyway.

And here she was again.

Walking behind it now, Sylvie squatted down to piss, watching the road.

As she finished, she saw a cloud of dust rising, a spot where the horizon blurred. She stood up too quickly, piss dribbling down her thigh. Someone was coming. She got back into the car and started the engine.

Sylvie's dad, Joe, ran a caravan park for old people. People like him, basically, who had lost their jobs or their families, or whose families couldn't afford to look after them anymore. Joe liked to say this was his contribution to the resistance. Many of the residents, or so he claimed, were members of organisations that were now illegal. But Sylvie had been out there four years ago, and as far as she could tell, it was just old people sitting around smoking weed and playing computer games.

That last visit hadn't ended well, for reasons she didn't remember. She'd stormed off without saying goodbye. Since then, her dad had called her a few times a year, 'just to say hi', as he always said. No video, of course. Just his slightly altered voice sounding far away and drunk.

'So, hi,' she would say, letting the silence linger between them.

The last time she'd seen him was Christmas Eve, two years ago. That had been his idea. Surprisingly, her mum had agreed. And so they had all sat there, like a real family, with the windows open in her mum's darkened kitchen in Melbourne, listening to the dull pop of fireworks. Sarah had put up fairy lights and was wearing those Tibetan-yellow leggings Sylvie had bought for her, and which she saved for certain occasions. They ate Indonesian take-away and got drunk on drinks Sylvie invented with whatever she could find in the kitchen and the half-bottle of gin her dad had brought. The mosquitoes feasted on them. Her dad gave her a big, obviously second-hand book about Caravaggio, whose paintings she had liked as a teenager. The whole thing was weird. She had no memory of her parents actually being together — her dad had left when she was four years old — but flickeringly that night, she'd almost been able to imagine it as she watched them pass an ancient vape pen back and forth across the table. It was comical and kind of pathetic. Her parents trying to remember things, but never agreeing about what they were. And then her dad had suddenly stood up to go. 'Fucking hell, Sarah,' he'd said, flushed. Something had been happening at a frequency that Sylvie had been oblivious to. Or maybe she was just too drunk. Her dad kissed her on the head, as if she were still a child. 'Bye, Vee,' he'd muttered. Then the door slammed. And sometime around midnight, Christmas morning, Sylvie had brushed her mother's hair away from her face while Sarah vomited into the toilet.

Sylvie saw now that the approaching car was almost certainly military, and her heart thickened in her throat. The footage of police brutality couldn't be dismissed as deep fakes anymore, not since Aarav had been caught up in a night raid. Not since he'd been stripped and beaten and made to crawl on all fours along the road.

Now the car was close enough she saw what it was: a big armoured ute, with tinted windows, and soldiers with respirator masks sitting in rows in the back. Sylvie drove slowly, both hands on the wheel, like a person in an old movie. Then she heard the command overriding her own sound system, telling her to pull over.

She did.

The ute jerked to a stop diagonally opposite.

Silence. She closed her eyes for a second. The fear ran down through her chest. Badly, she wanted to shit.

Nothing happened.

Sylvie opened her window and heard the soldiers' voices, though she couldn't make out the words. Finally, two men jumped down and walked towards her. One of them stood in the middle of the road with his hands on his gun, while the other came to her window. He didn't lower his mask, but she could tell from his manner, from the side of his cheek, that he was just a kid. He smelt of cherry vape. She cut off boys like him in the bar all the time.

'Where you headed?' he asked.

'Melbourne.'

His eyes wandered over her. 'What are you doing in Esperance?'

'I was tired,' she said. 'The hotel back there hasn't been updated. I mean, the map hasn't.'

'Have you been in contact with anyone else since you left the highway?'

'Like who?'

His voice sharpened. 'Have you had un-augmented visual or physical contact with any other human-person since you left the highway?'

'No,' she said.

'Does this car belong to you, Ma'am?'

'Ma'am?' she said. She couldn't help herself.

The boy took a moment to evaluate this response.

'I won't repeat the question again. Does. This. Vehicle. Belong. To. You?'

'No, but …'

'Code yellow,' the boy said, and the other soldier raised his gun and pointed it at the windscreen, which may or may not have been bulletproof.

'You are not the owner of this vehicle, is that correct?'

'No,' she said again. 'I mean, yes. I am *not* the owner of this vehicle. It belongs to a friend of mine.'

She was still FaceVoiced for it — she knew that because it had recognised her — but she did not know whether she was still state-registered as an official driver.

'Step out of the car,' the boy said, 'and place your hands in the air.'

Slowly, she did what she was told.

The boy took out a small screen from his belt and held it up in front of her face.

'Recite the text,' he said.

Australia is a country that works together for strength and prosperity.

She said the words, making her voice rise at the end, to indicate what she hoped would sound like a question. Then they waited while her FaceVoice was processed. The boy watched the screen and sniffed. His eyes darted to hers and then away again. The hair follicles where his beard was developing along his neck were dark and widely spaced. He sniffed again. He seemed to have a cold. There was a buzzing noise. He stepped back and adjusted his crotch.

'That's been approved,' he said. He nodded. 'Stand down.'

The other man lowered his gun.

'Have a pleasant afternoon.'

The soldiers sauntered away, and Sylvie got back into the car and started the engine. Then she drove slowly past them. Behind her, in the rearview mirror, the soldiers climbed up into the back of the ute, which revved its engine and lurched off into the dust. Soon it was the size of a black bug, and then it was gone. Sylvie drove without thinking for what felt like a long time. Beside the road, waiting to be assembled, the enormous propeller blades of wind turbines lay like sacrificial swords the size of aeroplanes. Then she took the exit and rejoined the highway. She set the map and flicked back to autopilot. At last she found herself breathing again, though her hands were still shaking, and for a long time she allowed herself to be carried along without music or Vista, without anything to modify her sense of terror and relief. The day had become brown and overcast, and the highway was enclosed by great, fuck-off new ThermaWalls. Blind trucks and buses hurtled past, and, less frequently, the smaller government buses, which were crowded and brightly lit.

Scrolling through the Vista menu at last, she chose *India — Beach Road — Kerala — Afternoon*, and the highway around her immediately vanished. Now dappled light flooded the interior of the car, and little beachside villages, scrubbed of people, flowed gorgeously across the windows.

She cued up some music, Brainchild's *Sorrowful Songs*. But it was too sorrowful. She found something lighter, the latest Alcatraz D.I.Y., and set the temperature. Finally, she sent her dad a message:

I'm 2 hours away. Keep my dinner warm.

It was a sort of joke, but it made her wonder what *would* happen. Would her dad cook? She imagined something cold and stew-like, like dog food plonked out of a can. And what would she feel, seeing him again? She prepared herself to look him in the eye, without subterfuge or apology. Without bitterness. With only mild disappointment. Like an adult.

In what she thought of as her earliest memory, her dad was carrying her on his shoulders through a crowd. She must have been four years old, because not long after this, he'd gone off to look after an old friend of his who was dying in India. His 'breakdown period', as her mother referred to it. Her dad did not use this term. But the friend he'd gone to see had not died easily; it had dragged on and on, and her father hadn't come back for almost six months. Sarah had never forgiven him. Of course, Sylvie sided with her mother — she would have done so in any situation — though it was a tired old story, which induced no emotion now. Since that time, her dad had been in and out of her life, but when she thought of him these days, she often recalled, rather than anything physical about him, just the title of a book she'd found beside his bed during one of those phases as a teenager, when she had tried to live

212

with him: *An Area of Darkness.*

Feeling luxuriously weary, Sylvie tried to will herself to remember something fresh about him that might illuminate the darkness she was driving towards. But she couldn't summon any urgency; the view of India floating across the windows — the flickering light through the palm trees, the sea just beyond reach — was too lovely, and no new memory came.

The closest living town to her dad was called Katamatite, and it was a shock to see it in the dusk when she turned off the Vista. Taking control of the car again, she drove slowly through the wide main street. She saw a supermarket, a pub, a boxing gym, a police station encased in wire, and a low, black, vandalised building, which had once been a disco and was still advertising its farewell-party prices from several years earlier. An enormous Australian flag hung limp in the middle of a roundabout, waiting for a hurricane to come and flutter it. None of this was familiar, and everything but the pub was sunk in darkness.

Her dad's property wasn't where she remembered it being, either. It was further away, in what was now desert, at the end of a frightening dirt road that ran for about seven kilometres from the edge of town. Sylvie clutched the steering wheel and peered at the white hollow her headlights made in the darkness. On either side of the road, she saw dark flecks that might have been kangaroos, and the burnt-out brown carcasses of old cars, like giant cicada shells. The road twisted and forked, glinting at the edges with garbage. At last there was a cold glow in the distance, which became a scattering of lights and then a cluster of small, low buildings surrounded by a sagging chain-link fence.

This was it.

She drove through the gate and parked on the gravel driveway. No one came to meet her.

She turned the engine off. Then she pressed a button and the heavy car door opened.

Outside, in the actual air, the world seemed weirdly two-dimensional. Sylvie stood for a while trying to see it properly again. It smelt oily and cold. From somewhere nearby, bursts of hard laughter came, and then the sound of coughing and spitting.

A single concrete room opposite said OFFICE.

'Dad?' she called out, walking towards it.

It had a barred window that had been blacked-out from the inside by a torn poster from last year's AFL grand final, but the door wasn't locked. Bracing herself for something truly horrible, she peered in. Slowly, a dark clutter of tools and books and old power-cords emerged. Plastic bags stuffed with who knows what. A filing cabinet. All of it coated in dust and smelling strongly of human filth. On the wall behind the desk there were more faded images of footballers, and a sign that explained, in big dot points, the importance of speaking kindly to children.

She went back to the car and called her dad. The phone rang out. She hated him. Then she tried again, and this time he answered.

'I'm ten minutes away,' he said cheerfully. 'Sit tight.'

So she did, with the doors locked, wishing that she had never come. While she waited, she logged back on and swished through a dozen videos. Buddhist monks were burning themselves alive again. Halo-Burger was hiring. The unofficial list of disappeared persons was up thirty-six to 1457. Frida had attached footage from Tuesday's seeker riots, but the footage had been banned in the time since she'd sent it, and the link now redirected to the government's 'State of Emergency' homepage. Catching herself, Sylvie dropped offline again.

'Are you aware of anti-trust evacuation procedure update 3.03?' the voice asked.

'Yes,' she lied.

'Are you familiar with your closest Emergency Gathering Location?'

'Yes.'

Sylvie closed her eyes and recited the secret mantra her yoga teacher had given her.

Finally, an orange ute pulled into the driveway, and a big brown dog leapt out, so big that, for half a second, Sylvie mistook it for a horse. Then a man climbed out from the other side. It was her dad.

He had long grey hair held in a loose ponytail, fluffy grey sideburns, and a stained checked shirt, undone too far and tucked into his jeans.

Sylvie got out of the car again, and he came towards her with his arms out.

'Look at this kid,' he said.

She accepted his dank embrace, unprepared for the powerful sourness of his body.

'Please don't pat me,' she told him.

They stood back from each other. He was shorter than her, and skinnier than she remembered — a wiry, ravaged little man — but even looking at him now, she found it hard to see him properly, as if he were out of focus. They were said to look alike — it had always disturbed her mother to have to see in Sylvie the glimmer of her ex-husband — but Sylvie couldn't understand how that could be true.

Joe whistled admiringly at the car. 'Coming up in the world,' he said.

She could only assume he knew it wasn't hers. But he didn't ask. Instead, he started to say something about the old family Subaru they'd had, and the endearing name she'd given to it, as a three-year-old. She knew the story because he told it often: before she was born onto the earth, she had once claimed, Sylvie and the Subaru used to live in the stars together, where they drank milk and ate chocolate biscuits.

Joe laughed. His coppery eyes looked wet. Sylvie turned away. He was drunk, she thought, or whatever he was.

'I'm actually really tired, Dad,' she said. 'Sorry. Can we do all this tomorrow?'

He coughed and stood back. 'Of course, mate, sure thing. Let me show you where you are.' Then he cleared some gunk from his throat and spat. 'Help yourself to whatever's in there,' he said. 'Should suit what you need, I reckon.'

But how would he know what she needed, she thought, when he'd never known?

They trudged down a gravel path lined on either side by the dark shapes of caravans and small shed-like buildings. The sound of computerised gunfire drifted on the cool air.

Joe seemed pleased, and he kept calling out 'Hello' to people Sylvie couldn't see, who invariably called out in return: 'G'day Joe,' in fearful, lonely voices that emanated from tiny rooms hidden behind curtains or towels, but which seemed to Sylvie to be coming from miles away, from the far end of long tunnels.

The dog — Buddha — ran ahead, pissing on things. Her owner had died, and Joe had adopted her almost a year ago. She really was an enormous animal. Her eyebrows had turned grey, and her tongue slapped at the side of her face.

'How many people live here now?' Sylvie asked, just to say something.

'We've got about eighty full-timers,' Joe said, 'and another dozen that come and go.'

The comparison was abruptly uncomfortable. Hadn't Sylvie done much the same thing? Cloistered herself off like this, in a tiny world that was bracing itself against the outside?

'It's still pretty basic,' Joe explained, 'but it works okay. When were you here last? Two years?'

'Four,' she said.

'Four, geez. Well, you can see how much it's changed. We grow a fair bit of food now. Turn's out the soil's not as bad as we thought, because the channel used to flood right up through here years ago. We actually could use a hand with some of that, if you're round? None of us are getting any younger, that's for sure. I'll take you over, show you what we need tomorrow.'

Sylvie grunted. She'd been here barely five minutes, and he'd already roped her into doing his gardening for him, though he still hadn't asked how she was.

'And what is it, Thursday today?' Joe continued. 'Because we've got a movie night tomorrow. We do it every Friday. Mostly the old stuff, but you should come along. It's a good night.'

He pointed out some other features as they walked: a toilet block, the hall where they showed the movies, and, beyond this, a slowly moving crop of alfalfa, disappearing like static into the darkness. 'That's us out there as well,' he said proudly.

Was this the old *all this will be yours one day* speech? She cringed at the thought. The land had once belonged to Joe's father, or to his grandfather, but she knew nothing about either of them, and anyway, she'd never felt much affection for rural Australia.

'And who died?' she asked. 'Do I get the death suite?'

'Nice old guy,' Joe said. 'Professor of something once upon a time. All very peaceful. Nothing to be afraid of.'

When they got there, Joe pointed the torch, and Sylvie saw that number seven wasn't actually a caravan. It was a small tin bungalow, with a sort of deck to one side and a metal fence around the deck. It might have been cute, she thought, if it didn't look as if it'd been kicked apart and abandoned years ago. One of the windows was taped up with black plastic, and a child's green bike lay buried in tall weeds nearby.

'Are there kids here?' she wondered aloud. 'I thought it was just old people.'

Joe laughed. 'Haven't seen a kid for a while,' he said. 'So yeah, you're right, I guess. It's mostly just us now.'

The dead and the dying, Sylvie thought.

Joe was still struggling with the lock when a large woman came limping out of the darkness.

'Scrat,' the woman said to Buddha, who ignored her.

The woman's name was Carla.

Joe put his hand on Sylvie's shoulder, and then took it away again as if he'd been stung. 'My daughter, Sylvie,' he said. 'Down from Sydney.'

'Yeah, I can tell.' Carla nodded unenthusiastically. 'What's happening?'

What Carla wanted was a new headset. 'Mine's fucked.' She looked expectantly at Sylvie. 'Where are you, love?' she said. 'You got one?'

'Leave her alone,' Joe said. 'I'll see what I can wrangle. But while I think of it, there's a new guy you should hassle who's good with that Xtended Reality stuff.'

'What guy?' Carla said accusingly.

'Guy in twenty-three — Kavan.'

'I've met him before, Joseph. Don't assume.'

Joe held up his hands in surrender. 'Okay, okay,' he laughed. 'Why don't you go ask him if he'll take a look, and I'll come see you in a bit. There's some fixing over in eleven, where Majid was. I don't have to do much, but I want it done. I've got someone coming out of prison tonight.'

Finally, he got the door open and turned back to Sylvie, holding the key up on its little orange tag. 'If you need anything, Vee, that's me over there,' he said, pointing towards the fence-line, where a bus was illuminated by a string of pale lights hanging between two gum trees.

It was sadder than she had imagined, that bus — an old petrol thing, more or less useless now as a vehicle. Looking at it, she felt something stir and settle inside her. Pity or dread, like a coin sinking into mud. Most of the windows had been boarded up, but near the back, pressed against the glass, she could make out piles of large fluffy toys.

Inside, the cabin seemed like it hadn't been cleaned for a long time, but also, as if someone had only just left. There was dust on everything, but the tiny fridge was surprisingly full. A more-or-less ripe apple and a very rotten tomato sat on the bench beside the sink. In one corner, there was a small bookshelf, filled with heavy old biographies of footballers, which Sylvie browsed perfunctorily, remembering a distant time — she might have been eleven or twelve — when she had gone with her dad to watch his football team get beaten in the rain. She remembered frightening groups of men lurching towards her down long concrete corridors.

She found the toilet, which hadn't been flushed. She flushed it and sat down. Nothing. This happened every time she came to see either of her parents. Should she shower? The narrow cubicle in front of her was unappealing, flecked with dark hairs. She decided yes, though. A brief gush of brownish, lukewarm water, which smelt like metal. Afterwards, feeling a bit better, she pulled back the bed covers and checked the sheets. They seemed ok. She lay down and spoke instinctively to her watch before she remembered. She was offline. With some difficulty, she managed to loosen the clasp, then she tossed it into her bag on the floor. Her wrist seemed naked now. She put her hands to her stomach and felt — strangely, for an instant — an almost compensatory sensation of companionship. Something was unfolding in there, imperceptibly. Outside, a tap was dripping into a bucket, and beyond that, she could hear the far-off sound of traffic from the highway, which might not have been traffic, which might have only been the wind in the trees. No, it was definitely traffic.

The wind rattled the flimsy tin walls. Without the internet, the night beyond seemed enormous and meaningless.

What would happen if she decided she wanted to keep it? Surely they wouldn't ask her to leave? Not after all the talk about homeless seekers, and squatters' rights? And what would Harlow do? And Frida? Was living with her mum really an option? She lay still, ran her tongue across the ulcer in her mouth.

Eventually, she fell asleep and dreamt. When she woke up, five hours later, nothing remained of the dream.

She could hear voices.

Flashing lights, the heavy thunk of car doors. The army.

She got out of bed and went to the window above the sink. But it wasn't the army. It was a white car. Her father was there. He was helping someone climb out from the back seat and into a wheelchair. An emaciated old woman. He began pushing the wheelchair. The woman's head was shaved, her eyes closed, and Sylvie was reminded suddenly of some sort of medieval procession she must have seen in an old film once, its dark, hysterical aura. In the yellow light, her father's face seemed ecstatic, even as the wheels struggled to turn properly in the gravel.

The next morning was hot, and loud with the noise of crows.

'Where am I?' Sylvie asked, but her watch was still switched off and didn't respond. There was the sound of someone hammering.

She was pregnant.

That's right. It was like falling off a cliff. Her stomach rose up into her head. She was at her dad's caravan park, and she was pregnant and the skin on her thighs and arms was itchy, too. She had been bitten in the night by god knows what. Still, she was grateful because, for the moment, she did not feel like vomiting.

She took a cold shower, dressed slowly in fresh black leggings and the same old black top from the day before yesterday, and then, in a burst of optimism, made herself an omelette, with the food she'd brought from home, but which, it turned out, she couldn't eat. She stood at the little sink instead, letting the spasms pass through her. On the other side of the window, a big gum threw cool shapes.

So, she should probably go find her dad, she thought when it had passed. That's why she was here, after all. Although beyond that, she wasn't sure why she was here. It's not like she wanted his advice. What she wanted all of a sudden, maybe, was just for him to not be so far away. Fine. So she should do that. If only it weren't always up to her. She put on her sunglasses, then changed her mind, took them off, and stepped down into the glare.

Walking through the camp, she saw again what she had seen only murkily in the darkness the night before: low buildings patched with blue plastic, caravans surrounded by rubble and furniture. Further off, on the other side of the perimeter fence, huge piles of garbage had been painted white.

She was sweating already. In the daylight, everything looked poorer but less frightening. Here and there, old men in shorts and baseball caps, like prematurely withered teenagers, were pushing shopping trolleys laden with beer and water.

She found her dad trying to fix a doorhandle in the communal toilet block. The bathroom was large, white-tiled, pungent but relatively clean. A cloud of small flies seemed to hang in the middle of the air.

'Fucking piece of shit,' Joe hissed. Then he turned and saw her. 'Oh, hi,' he smiled.

They walked over to the bus together, and Joe made tea on a little stove while Sylvie sat at a grubby table that had been installed behind the driver's seat. The bus was packed with books and tools and stuff, and it smelt like dog. A floral curtain separated this area from what must have been his bedroom at the back.

Joe was fumbling around with the tea. Over his shoulder, Sylvie saw a framed family photo from thirty years earlier, her mum and dad grinning awkwardly, with a fat, serious baby between them.

'How long you here, Vee?' Joe asked over his shoulder.

'I don't know. Couple of days, maybe?'

In her mind, she had imagined a sort of week-long offline holiday. No screens. No politics. No Harlow. A bubble of time, unconnected to anything. But the reality was proving to be something else. Then again, she still had to prepare herself for her mum, who would have her own idea about what Sylvie should do. Sylvie had always found it difficult to separate her mother's opinions from her own, especially at close range. She tended to become vague and tired as soon as she entered Sarah's house, which exasperated Sarah as much as it satisfied her desire to dote on her daughter and control her. This was one of the reasons Sylvie had moved to Sydney to study, a reckless decision she barely comprehended at the time and which she was still paying for now, both literally and figuratively. The money she made working three days a week designing virtual conference rooms barely covered her student-loan repayments. University, on the whole, had been a thoroughly unsatisfying experience, though she felt she should be grateful for it, now that things were so much worse. And, of course, she had met Frida and Harlow, and, in second year, Igor, who she'd started a band with that seemed, for a while, like it might take off. As the lead singer, Sylvie had found herself so nervous onstage that she preferred to keep her eyes closed the whole time, which people found endearing for whatever reason, and she had gained a minor cult-following; one amateur video from a festival gig had been viewed thirty-five million times. It was not a great song, but it was their most popular one, and there was the relative satisfaction of rhyming *open season* with *nether region*. 'You need to monetise that shit,' Frida had told her, not unseriously. But Sylvie never had. And then the band broke up. What had felt like the start of something good was actually the end. She no longer spoke to Igor. Now she worked two different bar jobs, on top of the design stuff.

If she wasn't going to 'keep doing' her singing, then the least she could do, her mother felt, would be to put her mind towards something useful. But what the fuck did that even mean? And who would employ her anyway? The industry was overstuffed with designers as it was, and fewer and fewer of them were actual human beings. She would have to study something else. But what? And how could she afford it? Almost inevitably, she and Sarah fought, and parted on strained terms. 'Look at the world,' Sarah would say. 'Does the world need more virtual chat-rooms?'

The answer to this question was: probably.

Yeah, she was looking forward to having that conversation again.

Joe set the cups on the table with a bowl of white sugar and a jar of powdered milk. Then he went to the fridge, took out a can of beer, and drank like someone in an ad who had been waiting a really long time.

Sylvie looked at the clock on the wall. It was almost nine in the morning.

'That clock's an hour slow,' Joe said, noticing her glance.

Finally, he sat and smiled shyly across the table at her, with his brown teeth. He looked dried out, she thought. When he scratched his arm, she saw bits of skin float up into the sunlight.

'We should do this more often,' Joe said, filling the cup in front of Sylvie.

Sylvie almost laughed. 'Oh yeah, ya reckon?'

The whole thing felt absurd to her, as if she were a little kid again, playing tea parties. She remembered doing that with him. No, actually she didn't. She remembered watching videos of them doing it. He used to play them all the time when she lived with him. They would sit down to watch a movie together, and he'd get lost in his archive of ancient home videos.

'Remember this bit?' he would say, laughing.

'I don't think it's healthy,' she'd tell him, 'to always be, like, watching yourself. You're probably really fucking me up.'

And he would laugh again, and say, yeah, she was probably right. 'We probably did fuck you up, didn't we? Do you feel fucked up?' And he would peer into her eyes, a mock doctor. 'You don't *look* very fucked up.'

'Can we just watch the movie, Dad, please.'

A typical exchange.

Sylvie fished out the teabag with her finger, added milk and sugar, and took a metallic sip.

'You know you can stay as long as you need,' Joe said.

She nodded. 'Thanks.'

But she didn't need anything from him. Whatever it was she needed, he couldn't give it to her. It was annoying that he thought he could, that he thought he was doing it already.

They talked haltingly about the riots, the blackouts, the housing crisis. Nothing personal. He didn't ask how her work was, or her life more generally, and she didn't offer. Nor did she mention what had happened to Aarav, or the soldiers who had stopped her on the way down.

'And how are *you* doing?' she asked.

'Oh, you know,' he said. His hip was gone, and his back was on the way. But otherwise he was fine.

No emotions. Only physical ailments. Only his. That's how they did it. It was all coming back to her now. The routine. She was powerless to swim against it, and eventually they fell silent.

On the wall, above the kettle, there was a black-and-white photo. Some old Indian bloke.

'Who's that? she asked. 'Your guru?'

Joe turned to see what she was talking about. 'Oh yeah.' He smiled. 'Bhagwan. Yeah. Dad got into him for a while.'

It took her a second to figure out who he was talking about. *His* dad. It had been a long time since she'd thought about *Joe's* father, or even considered the fact that he'd had one, once. She'd never met him, because he'd died before she was born.

'Guess there was *something* to it,' Joe said.

'To what?'

'Ahh, you know.' He shrugged. 'Bhagwan. The whole thing.'

Sylvie looked back at the picture. The guru looked nice, she thought, though he probably wasn't. He was probably some kind of sex offender.

They fell silent again.

'So, you know, I had this dream,' Joe said, apropos of nothing, as far as Sylvie could tell.

Here we go, she thought.

'This was while I was over there.'

'Over where?'

'India,' Joe said. 'You know. Kerala. I still remember it. I dreamt I was playing water polo. Not that I ever played water polo. Anyway. There was a whole bunch of us, we were in some kind of pond. And Bhagwan came walking past, there was a big sort of procession behind him, and the ball suddenly fell at his feet. Everyone was watching to see what would happen. He picked up the ball and he threw it to *me*. And there was this sort of moment when all eyes turned, you know.' Joe smiled. 'And I dropped the fucking ball.'

Sylvie blinked. 'Okay,' she said.

It was a mystery to her how her dad kept the place running. He was such an impractical person, someone whose clocks all ran at different times, if they ran at all. And yet before his 'breakdown', he had worked in an office, in a university. *Another universe*, she thought. Another dimension of time and space. He had worn clean clothes, and done whatever people did in jobs like that back then — administration, communications. Presumably he had not been stoned or drunk the whole time.

Someone was yelling outside.

Joe finished his beer, stood up, got another one from the fridge. Then he sat down again. He opened it and looked out the window. Wind in the dust. The yelling had stopped.

'It was too late though, wasn't it?' he said. 'I'm sorry how that ... You know, Vee. With your mum and I ... I wasn't. I didn't mean to get stuck over there. That wasn't what I was planning. Running off. But yeah. One sort of thing just led to another.'

Sylvie felt her face becoming hot. She definitely did not want to talk about this.

'Geez Dad, what do you want me to say?'

'I don't know, mate. Nothing, I s'pose. You don't have to say anything. I tried to fix it. But you know how your mum is. And I don't blame her. Well, I do blame her a bit. She's pretty fucking whatever, but it's not like we didn't try. We just couldn't figure it out, that's all. We did try.' He sniffed. 'Anyway,' he said cheerily, as if everything had finally been resolved. 'How's she doing? She okay?'

'Mum? She's fine,' Sylvie said. There was a strange taste in her mouth. 'She and Orlando are back together.'

'Oh right,' Joe said. 'Orlando.' He pulled at the loose skin on his neck, the long white hairs. 'Sounds handsome.'

He wasn't particularly. Old was what he was.

'Not as handsome as you,' she said.

'Well, obviously,' Joe beamed, and Sylvie couldn't help liking the web of lines that deepened at the edge of his eyes. Once upon a time she used to miss him so much that she would hide in the corner of her bedroom and hyperventilate.

'Speaking of very handsome blokes,' Joe said, 'what's the Harley Davidson man up to?'

'Harlow?'

'Yeah.'

'He's okay,' Sylvie said, and suddenly the prospect of telling her dad that she was pregnant seemed actually possible.

'There *is* something,' she said. 'He keeps calling.'

'Well, that's how it works, isn't it?' Joe said. 'Love and all that stuff. Anyway, you can't be too careful, and now I'm thinking about it …'

He stood up abruptly and went behind the curtain. Sylvie heard him moving things around. When he came back, he was carrying an old gun. A rifle.

'I wanted you to have this,' he said, placing it gently on the table between them. 'This was Dad's, too. Actually, it was *his* dad's before that. Not to get sentimental about it.'

Sylvie looked at the gun. Then she looked at Joe.

'What am I supposed to do with it?' she said. 'It doesn't look very practical.'

In fact, she felt viciously annoyed. The moment when she might have been able to confide in him was gone.

'Here,' he said, picking up the gun again and showing her how to use it.

It was about a hundred and fifty years old, and much heavier than she expected. It made loud, satisfying clunking noises. Joe put his arms around her, to demonstrate.

'I could take you out while you're here,' he offered. 'Plenty of roos.'

'Not a chance, Dad.'

'Well, I'd really like you to have it anyway. It'd mean a lot to me.'

She handed it back to him.

'I don't think so,' she said.

Afterwards, they took a tour of the farm. In the shade it was okay. The air was full of flies and the droning excitement of sports commentary coming from somebody's caravan. This had once been sheep country, cow country, Joe explained. Now it was just kangaroos and wild cats that somehow survived in the trashed lots that ran between the solar fields and the government grain farms. The land was so flat it was oppressive. Sylvie felt thirsty just looking at it. She missed the ocean. The white glare. The huge, deadly waves thumping her down like a hunk of weed.

They walked on and came to a rustling field of alfalfa, which ran at ankle height for about a hundred metres. It would need to be turned back through before they could start planting, Joe told her.

Sylvie was only half-listening.

They walked through the alfalfa. Then the plants stopped, and the land became dead paddock again, flat and dry and depressing. A thin, acrid smell drifted on the wind.

The first time he'd brought her out here, she remembered, the first time her mum had let him, Sylvie would have been six or seven years old. She and Joe used to play a game called 'Nobody loves me'. She would stand about here, she remembered, while her dad knelt in the distance, pretending to cry because nobody loved him. Then Sylvie had to run over and throw herself into his arms.

'I do,' she would say. 'I love you.'

Whose idea was that? she wondered.

Now, all around them lay big, evenly spaced stones.

'And this is our pretty little cemetery,' Joe said.

The stones were grave markers. The names were painted in clumsy, faded red and black letters.

'Actually, lots of these need to be redone,' Joe said. 'You studied art, Vee. That's a job you could do for us while you're here.'

'I studied corporate animation,' Sylvie said.

'Well, it's hardly the Mona Lisa I'm asking for.'

—

They walked back to the camp in silence and stopped at the vegetable garden where an old man and an old woman were kneeling in the dirt.

'Now if you want,' Joe said, 'we could use a hand turning the compost through this, so we can get the beans in before the real heat kicks in. We've got Ruth and Lenny here working on it, but they're pretty lazy, so they tend to cut corners.'

Ruth and Lenny looked up, squinting.

'Speak for yourself,' said Lenny.

'My daughter, Sylvie,' Joe said. 'Sylvie's from the city, so she doesn't know anything.'

'Spitting image,' said Ruth, taking off a blue baseball cap and wiping the sweat from her pale face.

'Pity her for that,' Joe said. 'But I'll leave you to it. And don't forget the movie tonight. This is the cultural event of the, you know. The week.'

Sylvie worked beside Ruth and Lenny for what felt like ten hours but was actually about an hour and a half. They were thin, strong, forgetful people in their seventies, and it was true, they did tend to cut corners. They groaned a lot, and Sylvie liked them, Ruth in particular, whose high, rounded eyebrows matched the deep furrows beneath her eyes and gave her an owlish look.

Ruth had taught English Literature at a university about a million years ago, she told Sylvie. Lenny had worked for the Department of Education before he was made redundant. They talked about soil quality, crop rotations, drought-resistant grains. They laughed that they'd been sent off to a Marxist re-education camp.

In the garden there was celery, spinach, carrots. There was kale and garlic. Further off there was an old pear tree. All of it looked dry and ragged on closer inspection. Maybe this had all been workable once, Sylvie thought, but now the battle was being lost. The sun seemed intent on killing everything.

Drowsy in the heat, her mind spat up disjointed memories. All the times she'd come out here were mixed together now. There had been an irrigation channel where she and her dad had swum, and an old red tinny that had swarmed with ants when they'd flipped it over on the bank. They used to lie on their backs and point up at things they saw in the clouds: rabbits, dinosaurs, bulbous faces. She was six. Or she was fifteen. Or she was twelve. Then, at some point, she'd stopped coming. The ants got into the sandwiches. And once, she had tried to hide some kind of treasure up in the pear tree. She tried to remember what it had been and couldn't.

But the question nagged at her, and when Ruth and Lenny finally stood up, groaning, and limped off to lunch, Sylvie went over to the pear tree and hauled herself up. It wasn't high. The bark was sharp. The blossom smelt softly foul. She had been maybe fifteen the last time she did this.

And then, in a little hole where two branches forked, she found it.

An old, rusty locket.

She unwedged it.

It had been hers. But before that it had belonged to her grandmother, Cath. Joe's mum.

She tried to open it, but she couldn't. It was rusted shut.

The rifle was lying on the bed when she got back to the cabin. Checking to see if it was loaded — it wasn't — she lay down next to it and watched the slowly moving brown curtain, which was golden now in places, where the hot afternoon sun was pressing through it.

Finally, she called Harlow.

'I took your mum's car,' she told him. 'You can tell her what you want. I need some space. I'm staying with my dad.'

'Your dad?' he said, trying to understand. 'Really?' He looked tired, but he was gentle with her, worried, grateful she was alright. His mum didn't need to find out about the car, he said. She wasn't due back for weeks.

'Thanks,' Sylvie said.

In the background, she could hear familiar music, familiar voices, a familiar dog barking at something. Harlow talked about what was happening at home, about Aarav. He was okay, Harlow said, he was recovering. Neither of them mentioned the obvious fact that was growing inside her, but every word felt cumbersome with the knowledge of it. Nor did she mention the gun that was lying beside her, or the red box of bullets, which she had spotted on the bedside table.

'I wish I could touch you,' Harlow said.

Sylvie was imagining going through their shared belongings, separating his from hers.

'I love you,' Harlow tried, at last.

'Yeah,' she said. 'You too,' although she wasn't sure if she did, or even, really, what that meant.

To love someone else.

To *be* someone else, that's what she was thinking about. To be two people at once. To drag a tiny human filled with teeth and blood into the world, with your own body, against your will.

'Okay well, have fun then,' Harlow said. 'I mean, you know. Be okay. Call me. Try not to crash the car.'

—

Movie night was the only time of the week — other than the doctor's visit, every second Tuesday — when all the residents could gather together. Still, most of them clearly preferred not to, and there was only a dozen or so people scattered among the rows of plastic chairs, or eating dutifully at trestle tables in the corner, when Sylvie arrived at the hall. The room was humid, and smelt of fried garlic and cumin, which she found intensely unpleasant. She had not felt like eating with the residents of an old persons' home, and she was glad now of that decision.

Tonight's movie was called *Terminator 2*. Joe was standing in front of the screen, introducing it. He seemed to be enjoying himself.

'What we have here,' he said, 'is one of the great cinematic monsters of all time.'

'Yeah, yeah,' said Carla from the front row. 'Let's get this show on the road.'

A short, grim woman in a red dress said something into Joe's ear. This must be Deb, Sylvie figured, the woman Joe employed to help run the place, and with who, Sylvie suspected, he pursued some kind of on-again, off-again affair.

Old people continued limping back and forth, and one of them, a fat, bearded man, approached Sylvie.

Don't talk to me, she pleaded silently, knowing, of course, that he would.

The man smiled and eased himself down into the chair beside her. Ignoring Joe, who was still talking, he introduced himself. His name was James.

'I usually give flowers to ladies,' James said, 'but I only have this synthetic peyote.' He opened his hand to reveal a large blue tablet.

Sylvie almost laughed. 'No thanks,' she said.

James nodded ceremoniously. 'Bless you,' he said, as if she had sneezed. Then he sat back, closed his eyes, and began breathing heavily.

In the next row, Sylvie spotted Ruth sitting by herself. She got up and went to sit beside her.

'Hi,' Sylvie whispered.

Ruth smiled distantly, but it wasn't clear if she remembered who Sylvie was.

At the front of the room, Joe was still talking about the movie.

Without her baseball cap, Ruth's face struck Sylvie as being curiously unguarded, and she had a sudden urge to confide in her. 'I'm pregnant,' she wanted to tell her. 'I'm pregnant and I don't know what to do. Help me.' Of course, she said no such thing.

'Let me know if I can get you anything,' she offered instead.

Ruth's mouth opened and closed, but there was a sudden flurry of noise, and Sylvie couldn't hear what she was saying.

'You dickhead,' someone said to Buddha, who was making her way good-naturedly between the rows of chairs, knocking people's drinks over with her tail. She panted happily and put her big, stale snout onto Sylvie's lap for a second.

Then someone turned out the lights, and the movie began.

The main character was a robot from the future who befriended a young boy. Together, they tracked down the boy's mother and tried to save the world from other robots. The boy's mother had the same name as Sylvie's mother: Sarah.

'She's a real feisty fucking bitch, this one,' someone said.

And then, just when it looked like there was no hope for the heroes, Ruth reached out and took Sylvie's hand in her own. Her fingers were gnarled and cold. They watched the rest of the movie like that, without moving from each other, even after their palms had begun to sweat.

Back in the cabin later that night, Sylvie woke and, still half-asleep, pulled on her SkinSuit and fitted the headset. Then she lay down on the bed again and whispered Harlow a message.

'I want you.'

It was after two in the morning, but he responded within seconds.

'Hang on. Yes.'

She adjusted the headset, logged in, scrolled through the tedious permission options and waited. The suit was filled with tiny rubber nodes, which bristled in anticipation. Now she was awake, did she even feel like this anymore? But yes, she did. Or if not exactly this, then something like it, anyway. She chose a room in Venice, with an immensely high ceiling. She clicked *Afternoon*. The light changed. The sound of water lapped outside the slightly blurry window in her peripheral vision. The headset wasn't very comfortable, but at least she didn't have to think about the walls of the cabin. She did not have to think about the bed she was actually lying on, or the person who had probably died there. That was definitely not what she was thinking about.

'Okay,' she heard Harlow say eventually. Then finally they were synced, and Harlow was there, tethered to one of his less absurd avatars, but which still made him look like a Brazilian martial artist. He was pressing into her, which was nice. It was him, but not him, which was fine. She would have liked to kiss him, but that was not something the suit was able to replicate.

'Should we request Frida?' Harlow asked.

'No,' Sylvie said. 'No. I just want you.'

And it *was* nice to feel him, to see him, even though her suit hadn't been updated for a while, and there were little glitches — his image lagging, while the sensations moved on. A church bell tolled from the piazza on the other side of the little canal. A boat went past, a man in it was singing.

'Like this?' Harlow said, his voice sputtery in her ear.

Like what? she wanted to say. It wasn't really clear what he was doing.

Then he slipped down between her legs, and she felt the imperfect movements of his fingers cascading through her.

Sylvie lay awake for a long time afterwards, Harlow gone, the SkinSuit dumped at the bottom of the shower. She tried to concentrate on her heartbeat, but that only made things worse. Her heart was the source of the panic. From there, it stretched out into her arms.

Inside the locket was an image of a saint.

She had suddenly remembered this, as she lay beneath Harlow's heavy avatar.

Joan of Arc probably, or Saint Cecilia preparing to be beheaded. The woman's eyes cast up to God in her abandonment.

There were a few teenage years there when Sylvie had been as fanatical about martyred saints as other girls were about phones and boys. But why? Something to do with suffering? Her own suffering lifted to a higher realm by association? Maybe. But she had also always just liked the idea of the past, of history. The funny clothes. The way everything must have felt just as real for them, just as non-negotiable, even though they had no internet or proper painkillers. The saints were something Cath had been into. Saints and angels. But what had Sylvie been trying to do up there in the pear tree with saints and angels? She could not remember the impulse that had compelled her. She still hadn't managed to open the locket, but she remembered pushing it into the little hole in the tree with her thumb. It was the perfect size.

She got up and opened the door of the cabin and stood in the cool air. It was very quiet outside. The old clock-radio read four-thirty in the morning. The hour when most people killed themselves. Or was that three-thirty? Anyway, the clock was probably wrong. She pulled on yesterday's clothes. Found her black jacket scrunched at the bottom of her bag. Her watch fell to the ground, but she left it where it was, without bothering to confirm the time. She walked out into the night, past her father's silent bus, past the pear tree and up towards the little cemetery.

It was colder than she had expected. Her feet crunched loudly on the gravel and the air smelt sweet with distant smoke. Now she could hear the ticking of insects, the sound of things living in bushes, a TV. The moon was almost full, the settlement lights at Tycho faintly visible on the lower rim.

After Cath's husband Bill died, Cath and Sylvie had driven up to Sydney together because Sylvie was going off the rails. That's what she'd heard her mum say. But she was only fifteen — of course she was going off the rails. She hadn't thought about that trip for a long time.

They'd stayed in old motels beside the highway and drank champagne every evening — two glasses for Cath and one for Sylvie — of the most expensive sort they could find.

Sylvie opened the gate and walked through the alfalfa, which swished pleasantly in the darkness. *Sooner or later*, she thought, *the fires will come through this place*. Fire or scavengers. There would be nothing they could do about it. And what was with that fucking gun he'd given her? The alfalfa ended and she kept going, stepping among the gravestones until she came to the place — more or less — where he used to kneel down and pretend to cry.

Now she knelt down herself and put her hands into the dry dirt. Then she took them out again, unsatisfied, and licked her fingers. The ulcer in her mouth stung but she enjoyed the pain, the bitter taste. She closed her eyes. Then she opened them. She was suddenly very thirsty. Further off, a meandering line of gum trees followed the creek. She remembered swimming there once, and saw an image of herself stooping to drink the clear water, like some sort of Pre-Raphaelite figure. That's what she would do. She stood up and began walking again. She was not cold anymore. There was the smell of eucalyptus. She was thinking about her grandmother Cath, and about the way Ruth had held her hand, and about the hand of the terminator as he'd disappeared into the molten steel. Thumbs up.

Something was lying in the dry grass at the edge of the trees. A dead bird, maybe. She walked towards it. The body of a large bird with its chest opened up, a chunk of the chest missing, the dull red cavity exposed. Putrefying and teeming with ants. There were wild cats out here, and what else? But it wasn't a bird, she realised when she got close enough to see. It was a blue baseball cap. Red on the inside. Lost.

With the logo of a beer company on the front.

She recognised it.

It was Ruth's hat.

Maybe.

She knelt down and touched it. The fear of animals was replaced by something worse. But there were probably thousands of identical hats. It was the type of hat that was given out for free at public events. Maybe everyone in the camp had one. She reached for her watch. But she'd left it in the cabin.

And then she saw the first man. He was naked.

Sylvie froze.

He was walking slowly through the trees up ahead, as if looking for something on the ground, his giant, furry belly tight as a drum.

Then behind him, also naked, a woman appeared.

It was Ruth. She wiped her mouth on her arm. Her eyes were wide. Her moon-coloured flesh was like waxy paper. She paid no attention to the man. Her face was wet. She was beautiful. She stepped very carefully through the trees. Not an owl so much as a deer, Sylvie thought. A strange deer-woman. She did not seem to notice Sylvie. Her gaze was fixed on something else.

Slowly, more people emerged from the shadows.

And then Sylvie realised.

Of course.

The synthetic peyote.

Nine, ten, eleven of them.

They were not all naked, but some were. They were like a herd of nocturnal animals who had lost all sense of direction, who had strayed too close to civilisation. They were going to die soon, Sylvie thought.

They were preparing themselves.

The procession, that's what it seemed like, passed by without noticing her. Sylvie watched them wander away, bewildered, along the edge of the creek.

She sat down where she was, at the foot of a tree.

'I'd like to go crazy before I die,' Sylvie's grandmother had told her once. They had been sitting on the balcony of a small country pub.

No worries there, Sylvie had thought.

Cath wore long, expensive, filthy dresses, and was very deaf.

'Anyway,' Cath continued, 'I'll be dead soon enough so, you know, feel free to tell me whatever you want.'

And so Sylvie had, eventually. It was like putting things into a locked box.

But something else had happened, too. She had not thought about this for years.

Driving back to Melbourne, Cath had nearly crashed the Volkswagen. 'Can you see them?' she'd cried, swerving into a petrol-station carpark.

Sylvie followed her grandmother's gaze up through the dirty windscreen.

'What? What?'

'Angels.'

They flooded the bleak sky above the KFC, apparently. Luminous, in their thousands.

Cath had wept.

Sylvie hadn't known what to say.

And a few months later, back in Melbourne, Cath suffered a massive stroke, then died.

—

Sylvie said goodbye to her dad at the office the next afternoon. They even hugged each other, and she did not pull away until he did. He smelt of alcohol and his own odour, almost familiar to her now. He didn't ask about the gun, which Sylvie had left lying on the bed in the cabin. Nor did he mention the gravestones, which she hadn't got round to repainting.

'I hope you'll be okay, Dad,' she said.

'Oh yeah, we'll be fine,' Joe said, raising his hand to shield his face from the sun. 'Nothing to worry about here, Vee.'

It had rained briefly and then stopped, and now the clouds were moving in two directions at once, fast, low grey ones beneath zones of slower pink. She looked away and when she looked up again, a kind of giant black kitten was floating ominously over the paddocks towards them. The kitten turned into a hand with seven outspread fingers, then dispersed, and vanished among massive, inarticulate layers to the east.

They stood in silence for a few seconds. Then the car door opened, and Sylvie got in.

Joe came over and leant on the open window. 'This really is a very nice car,' he said.

She started the engine.

'You know it's not mine, Dad.'

'I figured that, yeah. Harlow's?'

'Harlow's mum.'

He nodded. 'Very swish.'

There was another pause.

'I'm pregnant, Dad.'

'Okay,' he said, taking his arms off the window and standing back. 'Shit Vee, that's. What is that? You should have told me. We could've.

I don't know. Had a beer.'

'I'm telling you now.'

'Yeah, well, that's fantastic.'

He looked slightly stoned, certainly slightly drunk, but his smile seemed genuine. *That'll have to do*, she thought.

'Yep,' she said. 'It's fantastic. Thanks, Dad. Anyway. I guess I'll see you later.'

'Good for you, Vee,' he said. 'Love you, mate. Drive safe.' He tapped the car as she drove away.

In the rearview mirror she saw him for a second, a dark shape with his arm in the air, and then the whole camp slipped out of view, and she drove through dusty light for a while, unaccountably happy, with the windows open. For an instant she caught sight of the caravan park again — a cluster of low buildings, a tiny graveyard beneath a smear of pink sky. Then the dirt track ended at last, and she turned left, onto the main road, and drove back towards the living.

Acknowledgements

In the first edition of this book, I neglected to acknowledge the origin of the title, which I stole from Nick Cave. Thanks, Nick! And thanks for being the greatest! I'd also like to thank my auntie Viv, whose name somehow slipped out of those first acknowledgements, and who generously agreed to speak to me about her childhood and her memories of my dad.